POPPY PYM
and the
DOUBLE JINX

SCHOLASTIC

POPPY PYM
and the DOUBLE JINX
LAURA WOOD

Scholastic Children's Books
An imprint of Scholastic Ltd
Euston House, 24 Eversholt Street, London, NW1 1DB, UK
Registered office: Westfield Road, Southam, Warwickshire, CV47 0RA
SCHOLASTIC and associated logos are trademarks and/or
registered trademarks of Scholastic Inc.

First published in the UK by Scholastic Ltd, 2016

ISBN 978 1407 16346 8

A CIP catalogue record for this book
is available from the British Library.

Printed by CPI Group (UK) Ltd, Croydon, CR0 4YY
Papers used by Scholastic Children's Books are made
from wood grown in sustainable forests.

1 3 5 7 9 10 8 6 4 2

www.scholastic.co.uk

"Double, double toil and trouble;
fire burn, and cauldron bubble..."

For my pal Mary, who loves a good miser.
And for Lena, Poppy's first friend.

Welcome to
BRIMWELL

To Saint Smithen's
School

BUS

Town Hall

Dweeble's
Cars

Saint
Smithen's
Church

Veg 'n'
Stuff

Chelsea Bunn's
Bakery

N
W
E
S

Miss Mangold's Tea Room

Post Office

Rusty Bucket's Hardware Store

Sparkling Sadie's Costumery

Library

Brimwell Books

The Jolly Dragon Pub

Penny's Parlour

Playground

River Brim

CHAPTER ONE

It was late in the evening and I was soaring majestically through the air, whizzing around like an acrobatic bumblebee. Somewhere below I could hear a crowd of people chanting my name as I tumbled into a particularly impressive mid-air pirouette. Madame Pym, ringleader and trapeze-artist extraordinaire, swung back and forth in front of me, her short legs hooked over the trapeze and her arms held out waiting to pull me to safety. Reaching forward, I stretched out as far as I could, ready to grab on to Pym and to hear the humongous roar of applause fill my ears. Instead, I felt my fingertips brush Pym's before they slipped away, leaving me grabbing at nothing but thin air. Then I was falling. Down.

Down.
        D
            O
                W
                    N.

It was as if the world went into slow motion. The sound of the crowd disappeared and all I could hear was the thundering beat of my heart. With a sickening lurch of my stomach I saw the ground rising up to meet me. I opened my mouth to scream but no sound came out. Instead there was Pym's voice, full of fear and pain, shouting one word over and over again.

"POPPY!"

With a gasp I sat up in bed. My heart was hammering but as my eyes adjusted to the darkness I made out the reassuring shapes of my dorm room, and heard the gentle breathing of my two sleeping room-mates. I fumbled around on my nightstand and grabbed my torch, then I shuffled down under my bed covers and sat up so that I was inside my own little tent before turning on the light. I'd had the same dream a few times now, and sometimes the only thing that gets rid of those dark pesky nightmare feelings is a big shining light bulb.

*

Wasn't that a good beginning? I like it when a book starts right in the action with something scary like that. Don't worry though, there's lots of exciting non-dream stuff coming right up, and if you think about it, it wouldn't have been much good if that dream bit had been real. I mean, this would have been a very short book indeed – what with me being a total Poppy pancake. *My* favourite books are the Detective Dougie Valentine books by H.T. Maddox, and they're about this kid-detective, Dougie Valentine, and his dog, Snoops, and those books always start with him hanging off the side of a mountain staring helplessly into the evil face of the world's most dangerous criminal. Or something like that. They're so exciting, and I want my book to be exciting as well.

I have actually already written one very exciting book about my own adventures but my best friend, Ingrid – one of the snoring shapes next to me in the dorm – says that in a second book you still have to introduce everyone at the beginning in case someone hasn't read the first book. (But if you haven't read the first book you really definitely should. It got five out of five stars in my book group. I suppose I *should* say that my book group is just

3

me and The Magnificent Marvin, but still, you have to admit a top score like that is pretty impressive. We're quite picky, you know.) Anyway, allow me to introduce myself. My name is Poppy Pym and I'm eleven. When I was a baby a magician called The Magnificent Marvin pulled me out of his magic hat. I know how it sounds, but it's true! The only clue about where I had come from was a note pinned to my blankets that read:

This is my baby.
I know she will be happy here.
Please look after her.
~E

Well, whoever E is, they were right. I *have* been happy, because The Magnificent Marvin was a part of Madame Pym's Spectacular Travelling Circus, and I have lived there with my family of funny and eccentric performers ever since. There's Madame

Pym herself, of course, who also has psychic abilities (she has one good eye that seems to notice everything and one bad eye that screws up a bit and can see into the future. Pym says that's one eye for looking out and one for looking in), and The Magnificent Marvin, but a circus wouldn't be any good without a few more entertainers – and Madame Pym's circus is the best in the world. Marvin's wife Doris is his assistant, but she's also a tightrope walker and inventor, then there's Luigi the lion tamer and his lion, Buttercup; Tina and Tawna the horse-riding gymnasts, BoBo the happy clown and Chuckles the sad clown, Sharp-Eye Sheila the knife thrower, Boris Von Jurgen the strongman and last of all, Fanella the Italian snake-charmer and fire-eater, and her long orange snake, Otis. Still snuggled under my sheets I shone my torch on a photo of us all that had been taken a few weeks ago, after we recovered a priceless ruby scarab, and that took pride of place on my bedside table. I'll stick in a copy here so that if you haven't read about them before you can get to know everyone a bit better.

Now, you might be wondering why I was waking up in a dorm room if I grew up in a circus. (I knew you'd spot that, you beady-eyed brainiac.) What happened was that I recently started going to a swanky boarding school called Saint Smithen's. When I first arrived school felt huge and scary – I mean, it's a pretty big change, going from worrying about getting up in time to feed the lion, to getting up in time to attend a maths lesson – but Saint Smithen's had started to feel like home. Well, almost.

I shivered under my blankets, remembering my dream. It felt so real every time I had it. In the beginning I was always so happy to be back home at the circus, but by the end I was relieved to wake up and find myself at home at Saint Smithen's. (It's a funny word, "home", isn't it, when you've got more than one of them?) The dream was always the same – I would be performing high up on the trapeze and everything would be going brilliantly, the crowd would be going wild. Then, in the middle of the trick, I'd reach for Pym, miss and then fall to my certain death. (I don't like to think about that bit too much.) I wasn't sure why I kept having the dream, but in all of my favourite books it seemed like mysterious dreams usually came before big adventures. Well, maybe some of Pym's psychic powers were rubbing off on me, because as I turned off the torch and squished my eyes tight shut, trying to get back to sleep, I had the tingling feeling that a fresh mystery might be just around the corner.

And guess what? I was right.

(And I'll warn you right now ... it's a pretty spooky story. So maybe read it with the lights on.)

CHAPTER TWO

I must have drifted off to sleep for another couple of hours but I still woke up ages before my alarm clock was set to go off, when the first fingers of sunlight were just tugging at the edges of the curtains. I knew that I needed to banish the last of those scared feelings that seem to stick to you after a bad dream, and I had a great plan for how to do it. Trying to be as super stealthy as possible I pulled some green wellies on, and yanked a yellow coat over the top of my purple stripy pyjamas before making a break for it, down the stairs and into the chilly early morning air. As I scrunched along over the gravel path and between the towering ancient oak trees that stretched out in front of the school, the sun was just coming up, burning the sky like a beautiful flaming bowl of orange jelly. I wriggled my nose and took a deep breath of autumn air that smelled of crunchy leaves and bonfires and conker fights. With a quick look around to make sure there was no one else about, I turned a neat line of perfect cartwheels over the slightly dewy grass. Then I pushed myself forward into a series of flips, springing up higher and higher, the world spinning and righting itself around me like I was looking at it through a wonky kaleidoscope. I jumped in the air, tumbling and twirling, backwards and forwards until I was out of breath. Collapsing into a pillow of scrunchy orange leaves, I lay panting and pink cheeked, feeling my blood whirring around my body and my fingers and toes tingling. *That's better*, I thought. *Nothing like a bit of circus practice to make me feel like ME again.*

Once I had got my breath back I realized I would need to get a shuffle on if I didn't want to miss breakfast. Racing back along the path so fast that I was just a green, yellow and purple blur, I pushed through the entrance to the girls' dormitory and through a jumble of girls, tennis racquets, hockey sticks, musical instruments and football boots. I wound my way through the labyrinth of corridors until I came back to the door for our room, with its gleaming brass sign that reads GOLDFINCHES 3 in elegant letters. (The school is split into four houses: Goldfinches, Sparrows, Robins and Wrens. It's part of an old tradition and you can see all four house birds on the school crest. Apparently old Saint Smithen was a big fan of birds, but you'd have to ask Ingrid for the whole story on that one.) I share my room with Ingrid and Letty. They're brilliant. Ingrid is the cleverest person I know and the best pal you could ask for. Letty is a year older than us and she's like a human tornado – always on the move. She's in a LOT of different clubs and that means she's always off doing loads of different activities. Here's a picture of us in front of Saint Smithen's. That small boy pulling the funny face is Kip Kapur. He's my other best friend, and you shouldn't let his smallness fool you. He's got the biggest voice you ever heard. (And a big appetite to match.)

I pushed the door to my room open to find that Ingrid was already up, dressed and occupying her usual position: sitting neatly on her bed with a humongous book right in front of her short-sighted eyes. The title on the front of this one was *Ulysses*. It sounded like a book about someone sneezing to me, but it was *very* long so it was probably about some other stuff as well.

"Boo!" I said, not even that loudly. Ingrid leapt in the air and the book fell from her hands with a mighty, and slightly dusty, thump.

"Poppy!" she squeaked, "where have you been?"

"I went to do a bit of circus practice. Restless legs, you know," I said, tugging off my wellies and changing into my uniform as speedily as I could.

"Letty's already left for French club, but I wanted to wait for you before breakfast," Ingrid said. "Although, I didn't mind much because I *was* enjoying my book." She looked wistfully towards the fat book lying on the floor and her giant eyes gleamed behind her spectacles. "I don't suppose there's time for me to just finish this chapter. . ." Her hands stretched towards it, like a thirsty person reaching for water.

I grabbed Ingrid's arm with a groan. "You must be

joking, Ing! I'm FAMISHED." I rubbed my stomach which was growling like a disgruntled lion cub. "I haven't had a BITE to eat since my double-chocolate fudge rainbow-sprinkle sundae. And that was well over twelve hours ago! They're practically starving us at this school! Let's go and get some breakfast."

We made our way outside, falling in with the steady stream of girls heading to the dining room.

"I had a letter from my mum and dad at the stamp collectors' fair," sighed Ingrid, pulling out a thin white envelope. "Their mint condition Penny Black is the star attraction. Plus apparently everyone keeps acting like they are celebrities because their new book *Stamps for Scamps: It's Never Too Early to Start Stamp Collecting* just came out."

(I suppose not every book can be as interesting as mine.)

"That's . . . er . . . nice," I said. I would never really understand Ingrid's parents' obsession with stamps, but then neither did Ingrid.

"Have you seen Kip yet this morning?" she asked, changing the subject.

"No," I said, shaking my head, "I came straight here, but he's hardly likely to miss his breakfast, is he?" We both squawked with laughter at that idea because it was so ridiculous, and we were proved right as we entered the main building and headed for the dining hall. We could hear his foghorn voice blasting over all the other muffled chatter.

". . . and I said, no, it's a PEANUT," Kip yelled at his startled-looking audience, laughing noisily at his own story. "Poppy! Ingrid! Over here!" he cried, waving both arms wildly in our direction as if otherwise we would have no idea he was around.

"Hey, Kip!" I said, punching him on the arm in a friendly way.

"I thought you guys were going to miss breakfast," Kip said, suddenly serious. "I got some extra bacon sandwiches just in case you were late but then I accidentally ate them all while I was busy telling this great story." His eyes looked down to the three empty cereal bar wrappers fluttering in front of him. "Oh, er, and these cereal bars too, I guess." He looked genuinely puzzled as if he had no memory of scoffing them.

"Well, at least you took the wrappers off this time," Ingrid said placidly. After all we were used to Kip hoovering up everything in sight, especially if he was telling a particularly involved story.

We were all chatting away when a voice

interrupted that sent shivers weaselling down my spine.

"Oh look, it's the freaks' table." I looked into the icy blue eyes of my number one arch nemesis, Annabelle Forthington-Smythe. Growing up in the circus might have meant I didn't have loads of friends, but it also meant that I had never before experienced having a number one arch nemesis either. Unfortunately that all changed when I met Annabelle. I couldn't understand what I had done that had made Annabelle Forthington-Smythe hate me on sight, but whatever it was we had since become mortal enemies. (Plus, she'd been horrible to Ingrid since they were in primary school together and that was more than enough to make her a baddy in my book.)

Kip was staring at Annabelle, his mouth slightly open and full of his neighbour's cereal bar. Ingrid was trying hard not to look bothered but a telltale pink flush was spreading across her pale cheeks.

"I guess I am a freak," I said thoughtfully. "After all, I can do this." I reached behind Ingrid's ear and pulled out a chocolate coin. Ingrid giggled and I passed her the chocolate. Then I reached behind Kip's ear and pulled out another coin. Needless to say Kip gobbled that so fast that I'm not completely sure he bothered to remove the gold foil.

There was a cheer and cries of "me next, me next" rang out around the table.

"Oh no," I said with a grin. "Annabelle next."

Annabelle's lips tightened as I leant towards her before she could protest. Putting my hand up to her ear, I pulled out a realistic-looking rubber spider, its thick, furry legs quivering. Annabelle shrieked as I dropped it on to her arm, and she nearly dropped her tray in fright.

"What's the matter, Annabelle, scared of a little toy?" I asked, scooping up the spider and waggling it around for my appreciative audience. There were more cheers, and I stood up to take a bow.

"You'll pay for that, Poppy Pym," Annabelle spat, her eyes flashing. Then, with a toss of her blonde ponytail, she swept off to a table in the corner with a gaggle of her friends.

"That was brilliant!" exclaimed Kip, holding out his hand, which I slapped in a happy high five.

"Yes. . ." said Ingrid with a small frown. "Although I'm not sure it's such a good idea to make her so mad."

"She's always cross like that," I said with a shrug,

but deep down I knew Ingrid was right and that winding up Annabelle wasn't the bests of plans. You never knew what she was going to do, but it was usually something dastardly and befitting of a real meanie .

"Wish I could think of something really good to say to her when she's being nasty like that," Kip mumbled through a mouthful of chocolate coin crumbs.

"I'm surprised you can't," I said. "Usually me and Ingrid can barely get a word in edgeways around you." I gave him a friendly jab in the ribs.

"It's because he has to choose between talking and eating," Ingrid said sweetly.

"OY!" Kip exclaimed, swallowing his last mouthful. "I don't know what you two are on about, I'm not that... RILEY! RILEY! OVER HERE! RILEY! IT'S ME, KIP! RILEYYYYYYYYYY!" Kip was blasting across the room to a red-headed boy carrying a clipboard who made his way over, a grin splitting his freckled face.

"All right, Kip!" He held out his right hand and the two boys did a sort of complicated handshake. "Hi, Poppy. Hi, Ingrid." He turned his smile on us. "Are you all excited about the party?"

"What party?" I asked.

"Haven't you heard?" His eyebrows shot up. "We're having a Halloween party during Parents' Weekend. Costumes and everything."

"YES!" exclaimed Kip. "I'm going to go as something REALLY scary like, like. . ."

"A vegetable?" asked Riley, nudging Kip in the ribs with his elbow. The two of them continued joking, but my attention had turned to Parents' Weekend. It was pretty simple really, a weekend where the students' parents were invited to visit the school, have a look around and do some fun activities. I suppose it was less simple, though, if you didn't exactly have parents. At least not two nice neat ones with names like "Mum" or "Dad". My thoughts were interrupted by Riley, moving on to a new subject.

"Anyway," he said, waving the clipboard in the air, "the party isn't what I came to ask you about, I'm here to see if you want to sign up for the coach to Brimwell tomorrow? It's the first years' turn, but spaces are limited."

All three of us jumped to our feet. You see, Brimwell is the town closest to Saint Smithen's (the school sits all big and fancy on top of a steep hill called "Beggar's Hill", and Brimwell is nestled snuggly at the bottom). At night you can see the twinkling lights of the town glittering like a precious jewel from the dormitory windows. Most importantly, you can use a trip into town to spend your pocket money and to eat giant slices of gooey chocolate cake at Miss Marigold's Tea Shop. Each year group takes it in turns to go, so I hadn't had a chance to go yet and I was VERY excited to sample this legendary cake for myself.

"Oooh, yes!" Ingrid's glasses practically fogged up with excitement. "We can go to the book shop."

"Forget the book shop," Kip said, his face lit up, his mind obviously working in the same direction as my own. "We can go to the CAKE SHOP."

"Sign us up!" I cried.

We scrawled our names at the bottom of the list and Riley moved on to the next table. I sat back with a happy sigh, pesky thoughts of Parents' Weekend replaced by much happier thoughts of baked goods. Little did I know that that trip to Brimwell would lead to something EVEN MORE important than a slice of chocolate cake.

CHAPTER THREE

The next morning found a group of excited first years, neatly lined up outside the main building. We were waiting under the fiery autumn leaves of the oak trees that lined the drive, next to an old stone sundial that was decorated with engravings of acorns and oak leaves. I ran my finger over the engravings and worked out that the shadows said ten o'clock exactly. Glancing around impatiently to see if I could spy the minibus I noticed that a lot of the other girls who were waiting were wearing purple badges with the letters QFF written on them in glittering gold. I turned to Jacinta, a girl from my class, who was standing in line next to me, and asked her what the badges were. She clutched her own badge and giggled squeakily. "QFF?" she replied. "It stands for 'Quest Friends Forever'. We're Lucas Quest's fan club."

I must have looked confused because she said the name again. Louder this time, and more slowly. "Loooooooocas Queeeessst."

"Who?" I asked.

"You really don't know?" It was her turn to look confused. "Lucas Quest? He's an actor? He was in the film *Love Vampire: Vampires in Love*? And there's going to be a SEQUEL, *Love Vampire 2: Vampires More in Love than Ever*!" Her voice was getting higher and higher as I didn't show any signs of suddenly understanding what she was talking about.

"Nope." I shook my head. "Sorry," I added because she looked so upset.

"I guess maybe he's not exactly world famous yet," Jacinta sighed. "But he WILL be soon, and we'll have been his fans from the very beginning. Soon QFF won't just be at Saint Smithen's ... we'll have members everywhere!" She pulled a photograph out of her pocket and put it in my hand. It had been torn out of a magazine and showed a boy with tanned skin and dark curly hair flopping into dark eyes. His smile showed off a set of very straight, very white teeth, and the caption underneath read "Brimwell's resident love vampire reveals his love of puppies." I didn't really understand what Jacinta was so worked up about but one look at her love-struck face and I knew I had to say something nice.

"I like his, er, ears," I said.

"You can have this if you want." Jacinta pressed the picture into my hand like it was a really precious gift. "I have sixteen more copies from the *Brimwell Bugle* in my room. Maybe you would like to join the fan club?"

"Er. Maybe," I muttered, looking at the boy in the picture. (I'll stick it in here for you to see if you can work out what all the fuss is about.)

"He's fourteen," she murmured as if I hadn't spoken, her eyes glazing over dreamily. "And he's sooooo handsome. He actually goes to Saint Smithen's, you know, and his brother Andrew is a fifth year here as well. Last term he was off school because he was FILMING. Isn't that so amazingly amazing? If only I had started school a year earlier I might have already MET him. We might be IN LOVE!" Jacinta's cheeks flushed and she raised a trembling hand to her face. "He's back now but he isn't coming back to school until next week because he's still being taught by a tutor." Her eyes took

on a moony look again. "But he's actually FROM Brimwell." She waved her arm in the direction of Brimwell and her eyes opened really wide as she stared down at the town, as if hoping to be able to spot him from all the way up here. "And now he's in town rehearsing for a play. Maybe we'll actually see him. IN THE FLESH." She quivered and looked a bit faint. "We're going to try and find out where he's rehearsing and see if we can get his autograph. He'll have to come out some time."

I tried to look like I was excited as well and Jacinta turned back to her friends.

"Have you heard of this Loo Cast person?" I whispered to Ingrid, who was standing the other side of me with her head buried in her book.

"It's Lucas," she said, not looking up. "I think he was in some rubbish films about werewolves for about five minutes."

"It's vampires," I said. "Or love. I'm not quite sure."

"It's funny, the way people get." Ingrid shook her head. "From what I hear he's hardly even in the films – I think he plays the main vampire's little brother or something – but people at this school act like he's such a big deal. Why don't you ask Annabelle, if you're so interested?" She snorted (a most un-Ingrid sound). "After all, she's the head of his fan club."

And sure enough, there was Annabelle at the front of the queue boasting the biggest badge of them all. Well, that was all I needed to know – if Annabelle was a fan then I didn't need to hear anything more about this Lucas Quest character. Anyway, at that moment the coach arrived on the scene and two teachers got out, causing a collective but muffled groan from Kip, Ingrid and me.

First of all there was Mr Grant who taught botany, which is the science of plants. He is tall and handsome with a fierce-looking scar down the side of his face. Rumour has it that he got the scar while wrestling a crocodile on one of his many exploring adventures. As usual he was wearing loose khaki trousers and a dark green shirt, as well as a pretty excellent wide-brimmed brown hat. He looked exactly like an explorer from a story. But Mr Grant wasn't the reason for our dismay. That particular honour belonged to the lady standing next to him. Small and neat, with pale blonde hair and cool green eyes, Miss Susan the chemistry teacher was not exactly my favourite person, and I wasn't exactly hers. She had actually thawed out a bit since that one time I accidentally accused her of being a jewel thief (it's a long story), but she still didn't seem especially happy to see us. In fact her eyes lingered on me for a moment and her cold stare sent an icy shiver through me, like a hasty gulp of milkshake.

"Right, children," Miss Susan said crisply, "as you get on the coach, please make sure that either Mr Grant or I have marked your name off on the register. We will meet you back at the bus stop at two o'clock precisely. Lateness will not be tolerated." She looked sharply in my direction as she said this, which I thought was a bit unfair. I was hardly ever late. My idea of time was just slighlty more ... *relaxed* than other people's. "Please remember," she continued, "that you are representatives of the school and that how you conduct yourselves reflects on the reputation of this fine institution. TRY to behave accordingly." Miss Susan's eyes seemed to bore into mine again.

"And have a good time!" grinned Mr Grant.

Miss Susan went a bit pink. "Yes, well, that as well," she said, and began marking names off the register in her hand as students bustled on to the coach.

When I got to the front of the line Miss Susan

looked at me with a frown.

"Poppy," she said, giving me a curt nod.

"Hello, Miss Susan," I muttered.

"How are you?" she asked stiffly.

I think my mouth must have dropped open. Was Miss Susan trying to . . . *chat*? "Er. I'm good," I stammered.

She nodded and her cool gaze met mine.

"I like your necklace," I said, trying to think of something friendly to say. Plus it really *was* a nice necklace, a light silver chain threaded with tiny pearls and a silver charm in the shape of a heart.

Miss Susan's hand went to the necklace and she thrust it back under the neckline of her shirt. Something shut up in her eyes like a telescope folding in on itself. "Poppy. I trrrrust you and your friends will manage to stay out of trouble for the next few short hours. I've got my eye on you, so none of your usual escapades." Her voice went a little bit frilly like it sometimes does when she's being extra bossy.

Anger welled up inside me, but at the same time I was almost relieved. No need to worry, folks; Miss Susan was back to her frosty self and it was business as usual. I was about to tell Miss Susan what I thought about her accusations, quite loudly, when Ingrid nudged me in the back and up the steps on to the coach.

When I was in my seat I turned to face her and Kip who had plonked down behind me. Before I could say anything Kip thrust his face in front of mine.

"Gosh, Poppy, your face is so red! You look like a strawberry lollipop."

"Didn't you hear what she said?" I gasped. "I mean, we practically saved the whole school from a madwoman and Miss Susan acts like *we're* the criminals."

"Don't worry about it." Ingrid shrugged, her nose already back in her book. "You know what she's like – why would you expect any different? Anyway, we're not going to get in any trouble so it doesn't matter, does it?"

I knew Ingrid was right but it didn't stop dark feelings towards Miss Susan simmering inside me like angry soup. However, I was swiftly distracted by the squeal of the coach starting up, and the rumble of us rolling down the gravel drive. We were off! Looking down at the town lying below, all thoughts of Miss Susan were replaced with thoughts of cake.

After all, a girl has to have her priorities.

CHAPTER FOUR

After a short drive we stepped off the bus and into the golden October sunshine. Directly in front of the bus stop was Brimwell Town Hall, a very grand old building that stood three storeys high. It was U-shaped and covered in lots of large windows with white frames. The roof was made up of three peaks, and on the top there was a clock tower, capped with a copper dome on which a grumpy looking weathercock swung around in the breeze. There were tidy gardens laid out at the front like a cosy patchwork quilt and tall maple trees stood either side of the hall, their leaves a blaze of red and orange. A small sign with the words:

"HOME OF THE BRIMWELL PLAYERS: THRILLS, SPILLS AND FUN FOR ALL THE FAMILY!"

written on it was dug into the ground.

"Shopping first?" Ingrid asked. "Or cake?"

"CAKE," came the big, hungry reply from me and Kip.

We made our way past Saint Smithen's church towards Miss Marigold's Tea Shop, which was only a short walk. On the high street running through the centre of Brimwell the shopfronts were bursting with Halloween-y goodness. There were loads of carved pumpkins with scary faces, black and orange streamers, and spiders and bats swaying in the breeze, dangling from bits of string. Outside the greengrocers, Veg-N-Stuff, there was even a giant pumpkin that some clever person had carved with a picture of a witch on a broomstick, resting on a bed of sparkling cobwebs. It was obvious that everyone was getting well and truly into the Halloween spirit, and I found myself humming the "Monster Mash" as we crunched our way down the leafy pavements.

Turning down a small cobbled side street we

arrived at Miss Marigold's. The teashop was a small, squat building made of round grey stones, with fat roses growing around the door. Outside, a sign in the shape of a cup and saucer with "Miss Marigold's Tea Rooms" written on it in swirly writing swung back and forth. When we pushed the door open a small brass bell tinkled like a merry bird and Miss Marigold bustled in from the back to greet us. We were the first people to get there so all eight tables in the front room were empty.

"Hello!" she said, with a wrinkly smile for each of us. "You're new faces – you must be first years. I'm Miss Marigold."

"Hello, Miss Marigold," we chorused.

(Nobody knows how old Miss Marigold is exactly, but she must be at least ninety. She's like a character in a fairy tale with curly, powdery-white hair and gold-rimmed spectacles on the end of her short nose. She brings the smell of freshly baked bread and flowery soap into the room with her, and always seems to have a ribbon-edged pinny tied around her stout waist.)

"Come over here and sit at my best table." She bustled us over to a table by the window. "Now, shall I put some tea on?" she asked, and she disappeared before we even had time to nod eagerly.

"What's this?" Kip asked, after Miss Marigold had left. In his hand was a small flyer.

Brimwell Players

DOUBLE, DOUBLE TOIL AND TROUBLE; FIRE BURN, AND CAULDRON BUBBLE!

JOIN THE BRIMWELL PLAYERS FOR A VERY SPECIAL HALLOWEEN PERFORMANCE OF

MACBETH

BY WILLIAM SHAKESPEARE   DIRECTED BY MAXWELL DANGERFIELD

WITH SPECIAL GUEST APPEARANCE BY BRIMWELL'S OWN **LUCAS QUEST!**

BRIMWELL TOWN HALL • 7PM, OCTOBER 31ST BOOK YOUR TICKETS NOW!

33

"Who are the Brimwell Players?" I asked.

"We're the town's amateur dramatic group," said Miss Marigold, returning with a fully loaded tea tray. "We put on all sorts of productions in the town hall. Quite good, we are. We did *Frankenstein* last year. Gave half the town nightmares for a week." She put the tray down on the table and made a slightly queasy face. "Still, that could have had more to do with Magda's Halloween punch. Lethal stuff." She shook her head and glanced at the dainty gold watch around her wrist. "We've got a rehearsal at the town hall in an hour as it happens, so it's a good thing you came when you did or I would have been closed." She bustled off again.

Kip gasped at this near disaster, clutching at the tablecloth. "See!" he exclaimed. "That's why I'm always saying, MAKE SURE YOU GET THE FOOD FIRST. Priorities, people. Imagine if we'd turned up and Miss Marigold's had been shut." He closed his eyes and shuddered.

I patted his arm reassuringly and Ingrid poured out three mugs of gently steaming golden tea which seemed to revive him a little. Once the slightly green tinge had left his face, he looked down again at the flyer.

"So, *Macbeth*?" said Kip. "What's that about then?"

"Oh Kip," breathed Ingrid, "it's *wonderful*. It's about this Scottish general who schemes to advance his political career."

"Oh right," Kip said, looking disappointed. "That sounds . . . exciting."

"It's full of murder!" Ingrid continued. "And witches and ghosts!"

Kip perked up at that.

"Wow! That sounds great!" I said, slurping my sweet tea. "I wonder if we could come and see it? Maybe the school would do a trip?"

We were interrupted then by the gentle squeak-squeak-squeak of the cake trolley being rolled towards us. (Surely there is no better sound in the whole wide world than a fully loaded moving table full of cake being wheeled in your direction.) Kip's eyes grew wide at the sight of the trolley heaving beneath the weight of all the spectacular cakery. There was cherry cake with thick pink icing, an enormous gooey chocolate cake, vanilla cake covered in lots of tiny violet flowers and sugary rose petals, a triple-layered, heart-shaped Victoria sponge, a multi-coloured rainbow cake with blueberry icing, sticky flapjacks, giant chocolate chip biscuits and fat, sultana-spotted scones with jam and cream.

An awed silence fell over our table as the three of us beheld this wondrous sight.

"Well," said Miss Marigold with a smile, "what will it be first?"

*

An hour later, and stuffed to bursting, we waddled out of Miss Marigold's.

"Oooooh!" I exclaimed, rubbing my stomach. "I feel so full, I'll never eat again!"

"I dunno." Kip's voice was thoughtful. "I reckon I could have fitted in another biscuit or two."

"What, on top of the other five?" Ingrid asked.

Kip burped quietly. "Maybe just another sliver of cake. . ." His eyes went all starry.

Miss Marigold cut Kip's daydreams short by closing up the shop behind us and leaving for her rehearsal, much to the dismay of several students who had just arrived. ("FOOLS!" gloated Kip.) We called in to Brimwell Books next, and Ingrid and I fell silent, staring up at the walls of beautiful books. We spent ages pulling them down from the shelves, stroking their covers and reading the backs. I bought the latest Dougie

Valentine mystery with my pocket money, and had to stop myself from curling up right there on the shop floor and getting stuck in. Kip walked out with a *Bumper Book of Practical Jokes*, which I eyed nervously.

"Don't worry, Pops," Kip grinned evilly. "I'll leave you and Ingrid alone ... maybe." The manic cackle that followed made me think not.

Ingrid was bent double underneath a backpack full of book purchases. She read so fast that she needed a constant supply, and Mr B, who owned Brimwell Books, made a joke that Ingrid would single-handedly keep him in business. (I mean, he *thought* it was a joke, but to be honest it's probably more like what you would call "a fact".)

We wandered further into town, past Rusty Bucket's Hardware Store and into Sparkling Sadie's Costumery where a bundle of students were flicking through rails of Halloween costumes, eyeing up different options for the upcoming party. Ingrid and I admired the range of witches' hats, and I swept a healthy amount of fake blood, spray-in hair dye and face paint into my basket before taking it to the till to pay. I love a good Halloween costume and I was determined that mine would be as scary as possible.

"What do you think?" Kip's muffled voice asked through the rubber gorilla mask he had pulled on.

"I think it's a vast improvement!" Annabelle's voice tinkled from behind us where she and her friends were trying on fairy wings.

Kip lifted the mask and pulled a face at Annabelle. "I like your mask, Annabelle ... very scary!" he called over his shoulder as we walked to the door, and Annabelle's face scrunched up like an angry walnut.

"That was quick thinking!" I whispered admiringly.

"I know!" said Kip, looking slightly dazed by his own insult skills.

"We'd better head back to the coach," Ingrid said with a glance at her watch. "It's almost two o'clock."

We started in the direction of the bus stop, joining the stream of other students heading that way.

As we reached the top of the high street there was the sound of raised voices and someone rushed past us, running in the direction we were walking. Something was wrong. Up ahead we could hear people shouting and I wrinkled my nose, sniffing the air like a curious dog.

"Can you smell—" I began.

"Burning!" exclaimed Ingrid.

Kip pointed. "Is that—"

"Smoke!" Ingrid finished, and the three of us began hurrying towards the gathering crowd.

There, next to the bus stop, stood the Brimwell Town Hall.

And it was on fire.

CHAPTER FIVE

As we got closer we saw a group of people gathered, staring hopelessly up at the burning building. I felt my stomach drop towards my toes, as if I was looking down from the high wire. A billowing plume of dark smoke filled the air and flames were licking through the window frames of the second floor. The sound of breaking glass and the groans of the building were enough to let us know that there was no saving it; it was being gobbled up by the greedy flames. I heard a gasp next to me, and turned to see Kip and Ingrid's horror-struck faces as they stared up at the blaze.

Swivelling around, I spotted Miss Susan standing on the front lawn, her usually tidy hair standing out around her face and a long sooty smear down the side of her cheek.

"Miss!" I exclaimed, running up to her with Kip and Ingrid hot on my heels. "Is there anyone inside?" I asked, my hand grabbing on to her arm. I noticed that she was shaking and she seemed to look straight through me. "Miss!" I cried again.

"Poppy," she said in a muffled, half asleep voice. Her eyes came into focus on my face and she gave her head a little shake as if she was trying to wake herself up. "No," she said more crisply now. "Everyone is out. There was some sort of rehearsal on, I think, but Mr Grant and I were waiting here with the bus. Once we saw the smoke we ran in and managed to get everyone out." She gestured to the nearby group of bedraggled-looking people. They were huddled together and most were wearing the same dazed look as Miss Susan; some were crying. Mr Grant was there, making sure everyone was standing well back, and the front of his shirt also streaked black with soot. He was handing out bottles of water from the icebox on the school bus.

Most of the students had arrived by now to catch the bus, and we all stood in shock staring up at the fire. The sound of distant sirens alerted us that help was on its way.

I frowned. "How long ago did it start?" I asked Miss Susan. She was gazing at the building and she didn't seem to hear me. I repeated my question.

"It's only been a few minutes," she said shakily. "It ... it happened so fast. I suppose that's the way with these old buildings."

We were interrupted by the wail of sirens, announcing the arrival of two fire engines. Firefighters spilled out and swiftly began to tackle the blaze.

"Elaine!" called Mr Grant, gesturing to Miss Susan. She made her way over to his side and the two of them began to fill one of the firefighters in on what had happened. If it hadn't been so scary it would have been quite thrilling.

These thoughts were interrupted by a commotion behind me, and I looked to see a tall dark boy, who had been standing with the group from inside the town hall, slowly crumpling to the ground like a hefty sack of spuds.

A high-pitched shriek pierced the air – Annabelle. She sped forward towards the fallen boy. Flopping down beside him she cradled his head in her lap, weeping noisily over his unconscious form.

"He's – he's dead!" she wailed.

Miss Susan and the firefighter were moving towards the pair, but Ingrid beat them to it. With a flourish she grabbed one of the open bottles of water from someone's hand and emptied it over the boy's head, also drenching Annabelle who squealed angrily. She was distracted, however, by the boy's eyes fluttering open. He looked up at Annabelle and blinked.

"Th-th-thank you," he whispered in a weak voice.

Annabelle dissolved once again into noisy tears and Ingrid rolled her eyes before heading back to us.

"Pretty quick thinking, Ing!" Kip said, before throwing a disgusted glance at the tender scene that Annabelle and the boy were now acting out, staring deeply into each other's eyes. It was like something from a soppy film ... and with that thought, the penny dropped.

"That's that Loo Cast Quest!" I exclaimed, recognizing the boy from the photograph.

"Of course. He's in the production of *Macbeth* that they were rehearsing in the hall," said Ingrid thoughtfully.

"Urgh!" said Kip, eyeing the growing circle of Lucas's admirers, who were all staring moonily at his prone figure while Miss Susan asked him lots of questions about how he was feeling. "Dunno what all the fuss is about," Kip continued in his loud voice. "That *Love Vampire* film was so rubbish. I tried to watch it once but it made me feel a bit sick." He finished with a snort, but he looked a bit frightened when a host of angry Lucas Quest fan club eyes snapped in his direction.

However, there was no time to worry about Kip's personal safety because we were interrupted once again, this time by another scream breaking through the hubbub.

"BUTTONS!" A plump grey-haired lady was being held back by a firefighter as she tried to push her way into the burning building. "My Buttons! I need to get to him!" she cried, pointing to the roof of the burning hall. There, right up at the top of the clock tower on the roof of the town hall, a petrified-looking cat was clinging to the weathercock and mewling pitifully. "Oooh! My poor sweet kitty! The fire will spread and he'll be burnt to cinders!" the woman wailed, clasping her hands to her chest. "Buttons!" she whispered helplessly, fat tears rolling down her cheeks.

Well, I know it probably wasn't the most sensible

or well thought out plan in the world, but here was someone (or, more accurately, somecat) in trouble, and I knew that I, Poppy Pym, could save him. In the blink of an eye I was shinning up the maple tree that stood at the side of the building and that reached up to the roof. I could hear people shouting my name below but I knew perfectly well that the trick to being up so high was that you don't ever look down. After some more stealthy climbing I was level with the roof and I clambered up, nimbling along to the base of the clock tower. Taking a deep breath, I held out my arms to steady myself, trying not to think about the fire that I knew was creeping ever closer, or – the image suddenly flashed through my mind – the bad dream I kept having about falling. The flames hadn't yet reached the top floor but there was quite a bit of smoke and it was obvious I didn't have any time to waste.

"Come on, Buttons!" I clucked encouragingly, trying to sound calm and to keep the tremble out of my voice. I stretched one hand up towards him, but Buttons seemed to be paralysed with fear and so I took another deep breath and with only slightly wibbling knees I started to scramble up the clock tower itself. "Here kitty, kitty," I called again, and this time Buttons seemed to move towards me just a tiny bit. "Thaaaat's right," I crooned, "come on! Nearly . . . there. . ."

With a sudden and terrific MEOW, Buttons flung himself down the tower, bolted right past me and along the roof, and hurled himself down the tree, ending up in the arms of his frantic owner. "Thanks a lot," I muttered, backing up veeeeery slowly along the roof, holding my breath the whole time, as the smoke seemed to be rising up to meet me. I wasn't sure if it was my imagination, but I thought I could feel the heat from the flames curling around my feet. For a sickening moment I remembered my nightmare and the feeling of falling towards the floor. Gritting my teeth, and pushing those thoughts from my mind, I climbed back out on to the swaying tree branch and clambered down as quickly as I could to the sound of cheers below.

"Nice one, Poppy!" I heard Kip's voice bellow. When my feet were firmly back on the nice solid ground I found myself being pulled into a pretty uncomfortable group hug with the stout lady and Buttons the cat.

"Thank you, my dear, thank you!" the woman said, practically smothering me to death as she clutched me to her chest. "I can't thank you enough, and neither can my dear sweet little Buttons!" Like me, Buttons didn't seem to be enjoying the squishy hug very much and he was flailing around, meowing shrilly in my ear.

"No problem," I managed to gasp once I had disentangled myself from her grateful embrace.

"I am forever in your debt!" she cried dramatically, seeming to enjoy the attention from the crowd that had gathered around us.

"No, no," I stuttered. "Happy to help out."

"But you MUST allow me to thank you! You saved the life of my precious lickle baby-waby-kins!" She started making kissy faces at the poor squirming cat.

"No thanks necessary," I said quickly. "Anyway," I tried to change the subject, "you'd better get poor Buttons home after that adventure."

At that her attention snapped back to the mewling fur ball in her arms. "Yes, yes, quite right. Come on, my little Buttons-y Wuttons-y," she crooned as she shuffled off with the still-wriggling Buttons looking like he desperately wanted to make a break for it.

"Poor cat," I muttered and turned to find myself face to face with Miss Susan. She was shaking again, but one look at her pale, pinched face told me that this time it was because she was angry.

"Poppy," she said in a dangerously quiet voice. "Just exactly *what* did you think you were doing?"

"Well, miss," I began, "the cat was in trouble and I knew I could get up there very quickly—"

"Oh really?" Miss Susan interrupted sharply. "Do you know who else could have got up to that cat?" The look in her eyes warned me that she didn't really want an answer to that question. "How about one of these excellent firefighters?" She gestured towards the three fire engines that were now on the scene, and the firefighters who seemed to have managed to get the blaze under control. "There are quite a few of them around, I see. They're probably quite experienced when it comes to dealing with buildings being on fire. They could have even used one of those new-fangled inventions; perhaps you've heard of them? They're called LADDERS."

"I—" I began.

"I don't want to hear it," snapped Miss Susan. "Poppy Pym, playing the hero again. You were foolish and reckless and you put yourself in real danger. You leave me no choice..." And then she said the words I'd been dreading.

"When we get back to school, Miss Baxter will hear about this."

CHAPTER SIX

Miss Baxter is the headmistress at Saint Smithen's but she's not really like the sort of stern headmistress you usually read about in books. Miss Baxter has a round, friendly face covered in a smattering of freckles. Her hands always seem to be covered in ink stains, and her clothes are just crumpled enough to stop her from looking really smart. She is nice and kind and friendly – and that makes being in trouble with her so much worse.

And now I found myself sitting outside her office, in trouble yet again. I swung my legs, scuffing my feet against the polished floorboards. At the side of the room I was sitting in was a small desk where Miss Baxter's assistant usually sat and told you when you could go in to see her. Miss Baxter's assistant used to be an old lady called Gertrude but she was a bit too busy (what with being in prison and all) to answer the telephone and do all the other jobs that needed doing. Since then Miss Baxter hadn't managed to find a new assistant, and students never knew who they were going to meet, because a temping agency in Brimwell kept sending people up to fill in while the search for a replacement continued.

Today's assistant was a woman with stringy blonde hair. She was chewing gum very loudly and snapping it against her teeth. You could see it rolling around her mouth in a bright pink blob. She was staring into space with a vacant expression, obviously imagining herself far, far away from here. The phone on her desk buzzed and she picked it up.

"Yeah?" she said with a loud snap of her gum. There was a pause. "Yeah," she muttered again, clunking the phone back down. "You can go in now," she said to me with a shrug before resuming her daydream.

"OK, thanks," I mumbled, and with a deep breath I pushed open the door to Miss Baxter's office. In my short time at Saint Smithen's I had already spent quite a lot of time inside Miss Baxter's office, because even though I tried so hard to be good, trouble seemed to follow me around.

In one corner of the room a deep, comfy armchair was occupied, as usual, by Miss Baxter's sprawling orange cat, Marmalade. In the middle of the room and piled high with papers stood an enormous gleaming desk, and standing behind the desk at that particular moment was Miss Baxter.

As I stood in front of her, her normally smiling mouth was puckered in a serious expression, and I gulped. Looking closely I thought I could see just a glimmer of laughter lurking in her dark eyes. That gave me courage.

"Um, hello, Miss Baxter," I said, looking down at my feet before peeking up at her.

"Hello, Poppy," she said drily. "I was wondering if you would make it a full week before I'd be seeing you again. And it seems not." I bit my lip and looked back down at the floor. "Would you like a cup of tea?" Her question took me by surprise.

"Yes please," I squeaked.

"Have a seat," she said, gesturing to the chair in front of her desk before turning her attention to the tea set on a small table beside the armchair. After a moment she came over and handed me a china teacup and saucer with violets painted around the edges, then sat down behind her desk and looked at me over the top of her own teacup.

"So, Poppy. Why don't you tell me why you're here?" she asked.

I took a deep breath. "Um, well," I stuttered. "We were in Brimwell and … and you know there was a big fire." I paused here and Miss Baxter nodded. "Well, there was this cat on the roof and he was stuck so I just … went up to fetch him and then, when I came back down, Miss Susan was really angry. I don't think she likes it when I use my circus skills," I finished with a sigh.

There was another pause as Miss Baxter sipped her tea – and I tried not to slurp mine – and then she put her cup and saucer gently down on the desk in front of her. "I don't think it's that Miss Susan doesn't like you using your circus skills, Poppy," she said quite firmly. "It's that sometimes you use those skills in ways that aren't appropriate."

I put my own cup down and was about to protest when Miss Baxter cut me off with a wave of her hand. "No, Poppy. Miss Susan was quite right to be angry because you put yourself in real danger." She looked at me levelly. "And our most important job is to keep you safe. It all worked out OK this time, but I dread to think what might have happened." She shuddered and I could see that she was really concerned.

"I'm sorry," I said in a small voice.

"Believe it or not, I *do* understand, Poppy." Miss Baxter smiled ruefully. "I often used to get in trouble for rushing in without thinking myself, but in your case, your special talents can make that much more risky. I know we have a lot of rules here that you are not used to, but each and every one is there to protect you. It's important that you learn to follow them." She picked up a pen from her desk and rolled it between her fingers, looking thoughtful. "Your punishment will be to write a five-hundred-word essay on an aspect of Saint Smithen's history. Due on my desk next Monday." She leant back in her chair and crossed her arms.

I stifled a groan. It was not so bad as far as possible punishments went, but writing a boring essay was not exactly high up on my list of favourite things to do.

"Don't look so glum," laughed Miss Baxter. "You might learn something. But you'd better head off to the library." Seeing my still-miserable face Miss

Baxter attempted to change the subject. "Are you looking forward to seeing your family for Parents' Weekend?" she asked. "I understand they're all coming!"

I nodded. I knew Miss Baxter was trying to cheer me up, but to be honest thinking about Parents' Weekend made my insides feel wriggly.

Maybe it was being at a school full of students whose families were pretty different to mine (that was an understatement), but I had been thinking more and more about my real parents. Who was the mysterious "E" who had left me at the circus? And *why* had they left me behind? Leaving the circus to come to school meant that I spent a lot of time in a different world – a world where people had parents and ate cornflakes for breakfast and didn't start the day flying through the air on a trapeze. If I wanted to fit into this new world I felt like it meant being pulled further and further away from my circus family.

I was starting to have a lot of questions and I didn't even know where to start getting any answers. It made me feel a bit . . . lonely.

Miss Baxter must have seen that something was worrying me because she squeezed my hand. "If there's ever anything you need to talk about, Poppy, you know you can always come to me. I mean it."

I nodded and gave her a watery smile as I got up to leave. The trouble was, I didn't really know how to explain myself to Miss Baxter ... she belonged so firmly in the world of Saint Smithen's.

On my way out I passed Miss Baxter's temporary assistant again. This time she was on the phone and her feet were up on her desk. She was still punctuating her sentences with snaps of the pink gum. "Well, my Greg was there," she was saying loudly into the phone. "And he said there's no way the place should have gone up in flames so fast." She paused and blew an enormous pink bubble. I could hear the sound of someone squawking on the other end of the phone. "Exactly what I said," she hissed. "Dead suspicious. Seems like no accident to me." She noticed me watching her. "Can I help you?" she snapped, holding her hand over the bottom part of the phone.

"N-no, sorry," I mumbled.

She turned her attention back to her phone call and I walked slowly out of the door, straining my ears to see if I could overhear anything else.

"Sorry," the assistant said. "It was just some kid. They're everywhere here, it's gross."

The door swung shut behind me.

CHAPTER SEVEN

I decided to tackle my assignment for Miss Baxter another day, and headed for the first year common room where I knew Kip and Ingrid would be waiting. The thought of seeing them made me feel a bit more cheerful and I wondered how I could feel at all lonely when I had two such brilliant pals.

As I wandered over I thought about what Miss Baxter had said, about me putting myself in danger. I hadn't really thought about how dangerous saving Buttons might be at the time; I had just known that I could get to him so I had thrown myself in. Maybe scrambling on top of a building that was actually on fire without any kind of safety net wasn't my *best* plan. In fact, the more I turned it over in my mind, the more it made me think of the nightmares I had been having and the more sick I started to feel. I thought about Miss Susan's pale, pinched face and the worry in Miss Baxter's eyes and for the first time I felt guilty. And again I felt that familiar feeling in the pit of my stomach – that I wasn't like the other students. Would they have scaled a burning building? *Of course not*, my mind replied. Pushing through the doors of the common room I made a deal with myself to try to be more like everyone else.

When I arrived I saw that Kip and Ingrid had already bagged some comfy seats in the corner of the room, and once they had spotted me they jumped to their feet.

"Where have you been?!" wailed Kip. "You've been gone for hours! Did you get in loads of trouble? What happened?"

"It wasn't too bad," I said, flinging myself into a soft, squishy chair. "Miss Baxter was all right, but I have to write a boring essay all about the history of Saint Smithen's."

Kip groaned sympathetically but Ingrid's eyes lit up. "Oh, great!" she said enthusiastically. "I can help with that. It's so interesting."

"I'm not sure that you understand what that word actually means," Kip grunted.

"Well, the dictionary defines it as 'arousing curiosity or interest', but I can understand how *you* could be confused," Ingrid said.

There was a pause while Kip thought about this. Then – "Are you saying I'm boring?!" he yelled, and I giggled, sitting back and watching the two of them bicker. I felt my mouth stretch into a yawn, and I snuggled back in my chair, feeling warm and sleepy.

Before we knew it, our curfews were about to kick in and it was time we were in our rooms. It was dark outside by now, and hundreds of stars glimmered above us in the clear sky. The last thing I wanted was another telling-off today, so Ingrid and I said a quick goodbye to Kip and sped off to our dorm.

My head was buzzing, full of memories of the fire and the climb and Buttons and Lucas Quest – but when I climbed into my bed I felt suddenly as if my arms and legs were made of the heaviest metal on earth. (When I told her this Ingrid said I probably meant they felt like they were made of osmium.) It seemed a lifetime ago that we had all been waiting for the coach to go to Brimwell. What a day! I yawned an enormous yawn, one that came all the way up from my toes, and I caught Ingrid doing the same.

The door burst open and Letty whirled in like a spinning top, wearing a long red velvet cloak. She grinned, showing off a pair of pointy vampire fangs. "Had a good day?" she asked, spitting the teeth out into the palm of her hand.

"It was pretty busy," I murmured, too tired to question Letty's costume decisions. I felt my heavy eyelids closing. From her bed I could hear Ingrid's gentle snores.

"Well, just you wait for Miss Baxter's announcement tomorrow." I heard Letty chuckle. "You're going to be pretty busy for the foreseeable future, I reckon."

I wanted to ask her what she meant, but before I could even get the words out I had fallen into a deep and dreamless sleep.

CHAPTER EIGHT

When the alarm rang the next morning Letty was already gone (although I wasn't sure where – I had given up trying to keep her morning clubs straight a long time ago), and Ingrid and I bashed around getting ready before staggering downstairs to face another day.

The dining hall was full of sleepy early morning chatter only interrupted by the shrill brrrringing of the school bell telling us it was time for morning assembly. As we filed neatly into the great hall I suddenly remembered what Letty had said to me the night before about Miss Baxter having an announcement to make. (At least, I thought Letty had said that. It could have been a dream. Now that I thought about it more carefully, hadn't she been dressed as a vampire? *Definitely a dream*, I told myself.)

Miss Baxter walked out on to the stage at the front of the hall. "Good morning, everyone," she said, clapping her hands together. "Now, you're all in for a treat. I have an important announcement to make today."

OK, OK, maybe it wasn't a dream, I thought, making a mental note to ask Letty about the vampire get-up at a later date.

"As you all probably know by now, there was a very serious fire at the town hall in Brimwell yesterday," Miss Baxter continued, and everyone sat up a bit straighter. Of course the fire had been big news at Saint Smithen's and everyone wanted to know more about what went on. (Although once word got around that the fire had been nowhere near Miss Marigold's, people calmed down a *lot*.)

Miss Baxter glanced around the room, making sure that she had everyone's attention. "What you may not know is that the Brimwell Players were planning to stage a production of *Macbeth* at the town hall, on Halloween." (I think that quite a lot of people in the room *did* already know that, actually, thanks to their obsession with Lucas Quest.) "We have been approached by the play's director, Maxwell Dangerfield, and, after much discussion, we have decided to offer the school and this very stage as a venue for the performance, as well as all future rehearsals." There was a pause and you could practically hear the wheels turning in the heads of every member of Lucas Quest's fan club.

"Oh my gosh!" a voice squeaked, somewhere near the back of the room. "That means ... that means ... that Lucas Quest is coming ... HERE!"

A hullabaloo of squealing exploded through the hall.

Miss Baxter put two fingers to her mouth and let out a piercing whistle. "That is enough!" she said sharply. "Yes, I believe Mr Quest is connected to the play in a very *small* role, but more importantly he is a student here who will be returning to lessons next week anyway, following the completion of his work elsewhere."

("She means his work as a MOVIE STAR!" someone next to me whispered in a not-very-quiet kind of whisper.)

"He is not coming here to be mobbed. Any inappropriate behaviour will be dealt with most severely." Miss Baxter looked to the side of the stage and I noticed that Letty was standing there, although today she was wearing a neat, regulation uniform and her teeth looked perfectly normal and fang-free from where I was sitting. "Now," Miss Baxter continued, "as president of the drama society, Letty has her own announcement."

Letty climbed the steps and stood right in the centre of the stage. She took a deep breath. "My fellow students," she boomed dramatically, stretching out her arms towards us. "In solidarity with our fellow actors, the Saint Smithen's Drama Society, or the SSDS, has decided to cancel our own, one-woman production of *Dracula* –" (*Ahh. That explained the outfit*, I thought.) "And to offer our support to the Brimwell Players, I myself will be acting as stage manager for the production. I will be looking for further recruits to help backstage with make-up, props, scenery, that sort of thing. If you would like to volunteer then please see me after the assembly finishes." Letty's announcement was met with excited chatter. "I would like to add," she shouted over the noise, "that volunteers will not have access to Lucas Quest, so no time-wasters please – only those who are interested in the *artistic experience* need apply." Letty flung an arm in the air and swept into an elaborate bow. There was a short, uncertain smattering of applause.

"Yes, thank you, Letty." Miss Baxter gently patted her on the arm and Letty reluctantly left the stage. "It has also been agreed that all money raised by the production will go towards rebuilding the town hall," Miss Baxter added. "We are expecting a big crowd, thanks to the fire making the local news, and there is a lot of work to do so I would encourage you all to volunteer if you are able." With that, Miss Baxter smiled one of her big, crescent-moon smiles and said, "Now off to lessons, my brilliant students!"

"I've already put you three on the list," yelled Letty as we filed past her in the middle of a crowd of Lucas Quest fans. "First rehearsal is at four p.m., in here. Don't be late!"

"Oh, great," grumbled Kip. "Hanging around with a bunch of over-the-top *actors* – that's just what I wanted to do with my free time. Why is my life SO HARD?" He looked up to the skies and shook his fist.

"I think it sounds like fun," Ingrid murmured dreamily. "Maybe we could paint scenery or something – that wouldn't be so bad, Kip."

Kip didn't look too impressed. "We do enough of that in art class," he sulked. "Which, by the way, we're about to be late for if you two don't get a move on."

"Stop being so grumpy!" I laughed. "Working on the play will be fun. Maybe you'll get to be in charge of the swords or something." Kip did seem to perk up a little bit at that, and the three of us made our way upstairs to the art studio where our teacher Mr Jacobsen was waiting.

The art studio was an absolute riot of colour because Mr Jacobsen had told us to "express ourselves" on the walls last week and so they were covered in paint and glitter in every colour imaginable. Today Mr Jacobsen was standing in the middle of the room wearing a black polo-necked shirt and black trousers smeared with white paint. A flat black felt hat sat on top of his head and he was wearing glasses with thick, square black frames.

"Welcome, class!" he said, clapping his hands together. "Today we are going to be making collage pieces as a form of protest art. I want you to think about an issue you feel very strongly about and use your collage to create a visual representation of these feelings." He lifted up a large sheet of cardboard that was covered in words and pictures cut from newspapers and magazines. The words said things like INDUSTRY and WAR and HAIRCUTS.

"There are newspapers and magazines on every table," he continued waving his arm towards them. "So let your imagination run wild. Find something that you care about *passionately* and let that energy flow through you."

I pulled a newspaper towards me and held my scissors aloft, but I was stopped in my tracks by the front page.

THE BRIMWELL BUGLE

TOWN HALL FIRE: LUCAS QUEST TO THE RESCUE!

By Edwina Huffledown

Brimwell's beloved town hall was almost totally destroyed yesterday by a dramatic blaze. Experts on the scene say that they have not ruled out a deliberate act of arson. Witnesses report that the fire began on the second floor of the building where a local history exhibition was on display. The fire spread rapidly, inflicting terrible damage on the building which is 237 years old and considered a local landmark.

Caught up in the blaze was Brimwell's very own amateur dramatic society, the Brimwell Players, who were staging a rehearsal for their upcoming production of *Macbeth* – a play which, as most know, is often referred to as being cursed. While no one was seriously injured in the fire, several residents were admitted to hospital suffering from shock and minor injuries. Among these was local young star Lucas Quest, whose latest role was a small part in the film *Love Vampire: Vampires in Love* – a film that has been described as "the worst film ever made" and "like being forced to eat cold soggy cabbage for two hours", as well as "a crime against eyes" by some critics. (The movie's terrible reception has even put plans for a sequel in jeopardy, this reporter has heard, as production has been "temporarily halted".)

Witnesses on the scene report that Quest singlehandedly evacuated the building and saved a kitten from the inferno, before being rushed to hospital himself after suffering a fall. "He's a true hero," one young lady claimed, with another adding, "and totally dreamy as well." Quest certainly got a hero's welcome when leaving the hospital, and was greeted by fans and local reporters. Quest is quoted as saying "I'm just happy I could help. Some are calling me a hero. I don't know about that. I just think I was in the right

place at the right time, and then I did something really heroic. If that makes me a hero, then fine."

[Story cont'd on P.4]

"Look at this!" I hissed, pushing the paper towards Kip and Ingrid. Ingrid took it from me and Kip looked up from his collage which so far consisted of the word SALAD with a big red cross through it. They both began to read.

"That's not true!" exclaimed Ingrid, hotly. "You saved that cat, not Lucas."

"And Miss Susan and Mr Grant evacuated the hall," added Kip. "I knew that Lucas Quest was just a big show-off."

"Not that!" I said. "This!" I pointed to the top of the article. "*Experts on the scene say that they have not ruled out a deliberate act of arson.*"

"What does that mean?" asked Kip.

"That means the fire might not have been an accident. . ." said Ingrid.

"Yes!" I exclaimed. "I heard Miss Baxter's terrible assistant on the phone saying the same thing. I was just too distracted to realize it was important. But this confirms it!"

"Confirms what?" Ingrid wrinkled her nose.

"A mystery is afoot!" I cried.

"What's wrong with your foot?" asked Kip, looking nervously at my shoes. "And is it contagious?"

"No, not *my* foot," I huffed impatiently. "*Afoot*, as

71

in this is a mystery, starting right now."

"A mystery," Kip repeated. He seemed to be getting it now and his eyes widened.

"Yes, and it's one that we can solve," I crowed.

"I'm not sure this classifies as a mystery yet, Poppy." Ingrid frowned. "It doesn't say for *sure* that it wasn't just an accident. . ."

"But they haven't ruled out criminal activity," I said quickly, stabbing the paper with my finger. "And we were actually there! We saw it all – well, nearly all. There may already be valuable clues locked away in our brains." Kip peered at Ingrid's head as if he was waiting for a clue to fall out. "Plus," I added, "we'll get to be detectives again and investigate. It will be so much fun. Even if we only prove it *was* an accident then we'll still have done our jobs."

Kip was starting to look as excited as me. "Yeah," he said, thumping his fist on the table in front of him, "it's our next big case."

I could tell our enthusiasm was winning Ingrid over. "But where will our investigation start?" she asked.

"That's the best bit," I beamed. "We can start interviewing witnesses today. We'll be seeing everyone who was involved – because they'll all be at. . ."

"The rehearsal!" Ingrid and Kip chorused.

"Exactly," I said, twirling an imaginary moustache and feeling like a first-class detective. Looking at the newspaper in my hand I knew we had a case, and that it needed cracking wide open.

CHAPTER NINE

I was so excited about the rehearsal that time seemed to be going backwards. That wasn't really helped by having to suffer through double maths with Dr MacDougal. She is small and round with beetley eyebrows and the most flat, droning voice you've ever heard. That day her voice seemed flatter and droney-er than ever and I don't think I took in a single word. When Dr MacDougal asked me to "find x", I could only stare at her. It was right there next to her on the board. She had just written it down and she needed help finding it? I wondered if she needed glasses and so I tried not to make her feel bad by pretending that I didn't know where it was either.

Eventually though, and after what felt like several lifetimes had passed, the day of lessons came to an end. We still had an hour before rehearsal so I took the opportunity to give the circus a ring. I knew that I needed to fill them in on the fire, and on being in trouble with Miss Baxter again, but to be honest I wasn't exactly looking forward to explaining it all. Still, I thought, at least talking to them would take my mind off counting down to the rehearsal – and the phone was in the library, the perfect place to spend a free hour.

Let me describe the Saint Smithen's library for you, because it is maybe my favourite bit of the whole school. I bet if you saw it in real life you would think the same thing. It's enormous, and absolutely bursting with books for a start, but at the same time it's so warm and cosy and inviting. The high ceiling is painted with a mural of the sky, dotted with fat, candyfloss clouds that seem to drift around above your head. The wooden floorboards gleam dark and polished and there are cosy armchairs hidden in various nooks and corners, just crying out for you to curl up in them and lose yourself in one of the thousands of books crowding the walls.

Tucked away in the corner is a wall of old-fashioned pay phones that the students can use to call home, and this was where I was headed. There was no one around except for the librarian, Mr Fipps, who was humming away to himself as he lovingly sorted through piles of returned books. I lifted the phone receiver off the hook and carefully spun the dial around, calling a long number that I knew off by heart. Now I'm going to stick in a transcript of my phone call here for you to read. I like doing the phone conversations this way because it's like how Dougie Valentine does them in his books. It makes everything feel so important and official. The other reason I like it is because then you and your friends can have great fun reading it out like a script and doing all the voices. (Kip's Fanella impression is always especially excellent when we do that.)

Beginning of transcript
Phone rings
Long silence

Me: Hello?
Luigi: Ahem. Yes. Ah. Right. (Pause) What ho! The Flying Ferret here, reading you loud

and clear. Hotel business and whatnot at your service.

Me: Luigi?

Luigi: I say, that's jolly good. How on earth did you do that? Psychic powers, I presume? I know someone with the gift myself and she's rather extraordinary, but I don't think even she—

Me: Luigi, it's Poppy!

Luigi: Poppers! Oh, well that explains it then.

Me: Right. But, Luigi - why are you answering the phone? Where's Leaky Sue?

Luigi: (guilty pause) Who?

Me: What do you mean who?! Leaky Sue, the owner of the hotel; she always answers the phone. Luigi, what have you done with her?

Luigi: (voice gets a bit high and nervous) Now, Pops, no need to overreact! I haven't done anything with her. She's absolutely fine. Probably.

Me: What do you mean, probably?

Luigi: (hotly) Well it wasn't my fault, if that's what you were thinking. It was all Marvin, and now. . .

77

Clunking noises in background and muffled shouts

Luigi: (Muffled) What do you think you're doing? I was just talking to Poppy and you can't... OW! Let me go! Let me go!

Scuffling noises, sound of smashing

Fanella: Tomato? Is you?
Me: Yes, it's me. What is going on?!
Fanella: It is Marvin. He keel Leaky Sue.
Marvin: (shouting in the distance) I DID NOT KILL LEAKY SUE. OF COURSE I DIDN'T. DON'T TELL PEOPLE THAT.
Fanella: OK, OK, keep your shirts on. Tomato, he only PROBABLY keel her.

More clunking

Marvin: (panting) Don't listen to that madwoman, Poppy. Of course I didn't kill Leaky Sue... I have just ... temporarily misplaced her.

78

Me: Oh no, Marvin you didn't—

Marvin: Disappear her? Afraid so, Poppy. Of course it was an accident. But . . . I was distracted and I thought she was a lamp.

Me: A lamp? Well, can't you, you know, bring her back? Say the magic word?

Marvin: (miserably) That's the thing, you see, I've—

Fanella: (in background) HE FORGET, TOMATO! HE IS SILLY GOAT! HE FORGET HIS MAGIC WORD! HE STAND HERE SHOUTING "TURNIP! TURNIP! PARSNIP!" BUT NOTHING HAPPEN.

Marvin: I'm sure it's a word in the vegetable family. Anyway, I haven't forgotten! I've just . . . temporarily misplaced . . . err . . . beetroot! Carrot! ASPARAGUS!

Sound of door slamming open
Sound of phone being dropped

Leaky Sue: WAIT TIL I GET MY 'ANDS ON YOU, MARVIN!

Marvin: Leaky Sue! You're back!

Leaky Sue: BACK?! Yes, I bloomin' well am.

Marvin: Leaky Sue, I'm very sorry. You see.
I mistook you for a lamp—
Leaky Sue: A LAMP?!

Dangerous pause

Leaky Sue: I WILL 'AVE YOU KNOW THAT THIS
IS A VERY EXPENSIVE AND FASHIONABLE HAT,
LIKE WHAT THEY ARE WEARIN' IN PARIS AND
THE LIKE. I LOOK LIKE ONE OF THEM TOP
MODELS.
Marvin: (nervously) Yes, yes of course you
do. I see that now. It's just, you know,
the shape of it . . . and that fringe around
the bottom . . . it's a bit . . . lamp shadey.

Another dangerous pause
A piercing howl
Smashing sounds

Pym: Poppy, love?
Me: Pym!
Pym: FANELLA! PUT THAT LAMPSHADE DOWN!

Loud shrieking

80

Pym: Right, right, sorry, Leaky Sue. It's very ... fetching. I'm so sorry, Poppy, I think I'd better go and sort them all out. Was there anything you needed to tell me?

Me: (pause) Nope. Nothing at all.

Pym: Are you sure? I thought—

Smashing noises

Leaky Sue: I'LL DISAPPEAR YOU IN A MINUTE!

Luigi: Oh, I say, that's a good one! YOU'LL disappear HIM! Haha! I see what you did there!

Leaky Sue: PIPE DOWN, LION BOY, OR YOU'RE NEXT! I don't like the cut of your moustache!

Gasping noise

Luigi: How DARE you!

More scuffling

Pym: OK, I really do have to go now! I'm so sorry, Poppy, but at least we will see you

at Parents' Weekend. Say goodbye to Poppy,
everyone...

scuffling and smashing noises stop

Everyone: Byyyyyye, Poppy!

**scuffling and smashing noises start
again**
End of transcript

I put the phone down with a big pang of homesickness.
It was hard being away from the fun of the circus –
you never knew what crazy scheme my family would
come up with next and it was one of the things I loved
the most about them. I was also feeling a bit guilty that
I hadn't told Pym about the fire and about getting into
trouble ... again. I didn't usually keep things a secret
from Pym – well, with her visions it was pretty tough
to keep secrets from her even if you wanted to – but
she sounded like she had her hands full already and
I didn't want to worry her, plus a part of me didn't
think my circus family would really understand the
world of Saint Smithen's, or why rescuing a cat from a
burning building would get you in trouble in the first

place. It was a strange feeling to be doing something that was so separate from my family, and to feel like I was changing so that I could fit in at Saint Smithen's. Did that mean I was different from them? Did I still fit in as perfectly as I always had?

I'd tell Pym all about it when they turned up for Parents' Weekend, I decided, and I pushed any bad feelings that I had down to the bottom of my wriggling toes.

After all, I had a mystery to focus on!

CHAPTER TEN

After meeting up with Kip and Ingrid, the three of us rushed along to the great hall for our very first *Macbeth* rehearsal.

In the hall lots of people were already milling around. Letty was dashing about dressed head to toe in black and speaking into a walkie-talkie. "No, Craig, I said I wanted the stage to run red with the blood of a thousand armies . . . one bottle of red food colouring is NOT going to cut it." She rolled her eyes at me as she stalked past.

Kip and Ingrid were looking around anxiously, but I felt a flicker of excitement at all the hustle and bustle. It reminded me of rehearsing for a circus performance and that funny mixture of nervousness and excitement that gets stirred up in your belly. For once, I realized, I felt quite at home.

We stayed for a moment in the doorway and, looking around, I recognized a few people. I saw Miss Marigold who gave us a jaunty wave. We made our way over to say hello, and she introduced us to a tall stringy man. "This is Gary – he's our star!" Miss Marigold said, patting him on the shoulder. "Really wonderful, he is, in the leading role! He was born to play the bloodthirsty general."

Gary shrugged, a good-natured smile on his face. "I'm better at being a plumber," he said, "but being in the Brimwell Players is a lot of fun. Hopefully you lot will enjoy it... we're always on the lookout for new recruits if you're interested!"

We were all distracted then by the sight of Madame Patrice, the music teacher, who was wearing an eye-catching spangly leotard with a golden glittery design over a pair of purple leggings and shouting at a small man huddled over the school piano. "No, no, Jeffrey! It's five, six, seven, eight ... Jazz hands, jazz hands, double pirouette..." We watched as she took off, spinning around the room, her impossibly red hair glinting under the lights. Clamped in one of her hands was the empty cigarette holder she always carried and she put it to her mouth and inhaled deeply. "The theatre, darrrrrling!" she cried, catching my eye. "Doesn't it make you glad to be alive?"

Letty reappeared at our side. "Sorry about that," she said with another roll of her eyes. "So hard to find good help these days. From what I can tell the whole production was in a shambles long before the fire. It's lucky for them they've got a professional running the show now." Her walkie-talkie crackled and she whipped it out of her pocket looking alert and ready to spring into action. Nothing else happened and she put it away with a sigh.

"So what is it that you want us to do, Letty?" I asked.

"I thought you could help with props?" she suggested. "You'll have to make sure everyone has what they are supposed to have at the right time, and that the right props are onstage during the right scenes." She picked up three thick booklets from the table. "Here's a copy of the script," she said, heaving them into our waiting arms, "and I'll get you the list of what's needed." We followed her to the corner of the stage, which had its heavy red velvet curtains pulled shut.

Letty's walkie-talkie crackled again. "Letty? Letty?" a whining voice came from her pocket. "Letty, the mask you've asked me to find – I'm not sure what 'such as would make a grown man weep in terror' actually means ... Letttyyyyy? Are you there?" Letty gave a stifled groan of annoyance.

"I don't know how I can possibly be any clearer..." she hissed into the radio. "But I'll explain it once again. OK," she said to us, pinching the bridge of her nose between her thumb and forefinger and closing her eyes for a moment before turning to face us. "Before I go and deal with THAT crisis, here is the list of props we need." She handed Ingrid a sheet of paper. "Unfortunately, almost all of the props in the town hall were destroyed by the fire and need replacing. A few things were saved and they're in the entrance hall."

"But how are we going to find all of these?" asked Ingrid, pushing her glasses up her nose and peering at the list.

"I spoke to Miss Baxter and she said that we can use the props we usually use for school plays. So you three can go and track those down, while I have a word with Craig about a little thing called *artistic integrity*." With that, Letty turned abruptly on her heel and left the three of us huddled around the prop list.

"There's a lot of stuff on here." Kip frowned, running his finger down the list. "YES!" he exclaimed. "SWORDS!"

At that moment we were interrupted by the arrival of Lucas Quest. He wandered into the room wearing a thick coat, a scarf and a pair of gloves. Despite Miss Baxter's warning, he was immediately mobbed by squealing girls asking for autographs.

"Lucas!" boomed a big man in a lime-green tartan suit. He pushed through the gaggle of fans and slapped Lucas heartily on the shoulder before enthusiastically pumping his hand up and down in a vigorous handshake.

"Who's that?" I asked in a low voice.

"That is Derek Dweebles; he must be in the play as well," Ingrid answered in an equally low voice. "I've seen his photograph in the newspaper. He owns the car dealership in Brimwell." Derek Dweebles had a large red nose and impossibly black hair slicked back from his face with some sort of very shiny oil. Everything about him was big and loud. Lucas didn't look pleased to see him.

"Where have *you* been?" Derek Dweebles asked

him with a grin, digging his elbow into Lucas's side.

Lucas flinched. "What do you mean? I haven't been anywhere," he said quickly.

Dweebles chuckled. "And why are you wearing all that get-up?" he asked, pointing at Lucas's scarf and gloves. "Going incognito, were you?" He gave a loud honking laugh and an exaggerated wink.

Lucas smiled modestly. "I have a bit of a sore throat," he said, softly, a hand on his neck. "As an actor I must protect my voice, it is my instrument." He was distracted, however by the appearance of Annabelle.

"Oh great," I muttered. "Look who else has turned up."

"Hello, Lucas," Annabelle greeted him, with a toss of her blonde hair. "It's nice to see you again," she simpered.

Derek Dweebles chuckled. "Ah, young love! Are you here to help out with the play, dear?"

"No, I am not," snapped Annabelle. "I am here for a PRIVATE word with Lucas."

Lucas gave Dweebles a warm smile and a shrug before turning away for a more secluded, starry-eyed chat with Annabelle. A flicker of annoyance skipped across Dweebles's face, but it was quickly replaced with a broad grin.

"Ahhh, Mrs Khan!" he cried smarmily, bearing down on a lady who had just walked in. "Let's talk more about upgrading that old car of yours, shall we?" and he pulled her arm through his and bore her off around the room on an endless wave of chatter.

"Yuck," Kip said, eyeing Annabelle and Lucas like they were a plate of soggy carrots.

"Are you lot still standing here?" Letty's voice slammed into us as she scuttled past clutching a box of what looked like eyeballs. "All the prop boxes from the school are out in the entrance hall so you can make a start. Chop chop!"

The three of us began making our way over to the door. "There are a lot of people here," said Ingrid quietly as we passed by various members of the Brimwell Players. "And I suppose they must all be suspects. Where do we start our investigation?"

"If we want to work out if somebody set the fire on purpose, we need to find out if the fire benefitted anyone," I muttered. "The first rule of being a detective: establish a motive."

"So how are we going to work out who has a motive?" Kip asked.

I looked around the room. "We need to talk to more people," I said. "Gather more information." As we emerged into the entrance hall a figure caught my eye and I groaned under my breath. "And I think I know where we can start. Although it's not going to be much fun . . . we may be cuddled to death."

Kip and Ingrid turned in the direction I was looking. Standing in the middle of the room was someone who I knew had been at the town hall when the fire began, and she owned a cat named Buttons.

CHAPTER ELEVEN

"Um, hello!" I said, approaching the cat owner cautiously. She was busy sorting through costume rails with another older lady, whose curly grey hair had a faint blue tinge. "I'm not sure if you remember me..."

"My dear, dear girl!" she exclaimed, and pulled me into another smothering embrace. "I so hoped I would run into you here. Magda!" she exclaimed, turning to her friend. "This is the young lady that saved my Buttons!"

"My name's Poppy," I wheezed, rubbing my squished ribs.

"Poppy! How lovely! And these must be your friends!" She turned her attention to Kip and Ingrid who looked a little stunned.

"Kip and Ingrid. . ." I said, watching in horror as my two best pals were swept into their own bone-crunching cuddle.

"Ungaghgaha!" Kip's muffled splutters of protest drifted towards me. The woman released them and Kip stood, panting and red-faced, glaring at her with all his might.

"I don't think we were properly introduced in all the commotion," she clucked. "I'm Penelope Farthing, but you must call me Penny. Perhaps you've visited my little boutique in Brimwell? Penny's Parlour? We have the largest collection of cat-based collectables in the area." I noticed Penny's fluffy pink jumper had an enormous picture of a cat's face knitted on the front. "Admiring my jumper?" she said with a little twirl. "We carry them in a variety of sizes and colours – for you and your friends I would, of course, offer a ten per cent discount. . ." Kip's red face was starting to turn a sort of pale green. "I'm doing the costumes for the play," she explained proudly. And this is my dear friend, Magda, who is playing one of the witches," Penny continued. "Magda and her husband, Rusty, own the hardware shop."

"We also sell my handmade jewellery." Magda

beamed, sticking out a wrist on which a very ugly bracelet, that seemed to be made of a load of old bottle caps, was gleaming.

"How . . . lovely," I managed weakly.

Magda nodded earnestly. "One hundred per cent recycled materials," she said. "You'd never know this used to be a load of old bottle caps, would you?" We all shook our heads dutifully. "All the proceeds from my latest collection – 'bin bags' – will be going towards the town hall fund." She gestured around at all the hustle and bustle. "It's so nice to see everyone pitching in to support the play, especially after so many of the cast left after the fire. Well, they always say the Scottish play is a troubled production, don't they?"

"Do they?" I asked, confused.

"Yes." Magda nodded. "I'm not surprised that the fire scared off some of the more superstitious members. Anyway, everyone wants the play to do well, and to raise some money to rebuild the town hall." She looked sad for a moment. "It's terrible what happened to that building. It was so beautiful, and over two hundred years old. Such a tragic accident." she finished with a sigh.

"An accident," I murmured, sensing my

opportunity. "Yes. Although it said in the paper that it might not have been an accident, didn't it?"

Magda frowned. "I'm sure that was just the newspaper trying to make things sound even more dramatic. You know what those journalists are like. I can't believe that anyone would do such a terrible thing on purpose." Penny was clucking and shaking her head as well.

"Were you there as well, Magda?" Kip asked. "When it happened, I mean?"

"No I wasn't, thank goodness!" she exclaimed. "From what Penny says it was a very traumatic experience."

"Oh, it was terrible, terrible!" Penny shuddered.

"So were you actually inside when the fire started, Penny?" I asked breathlessly.

"Yes, I was." Penny nodded. "I'd gone in for a rehearsal. I'd taken my little Buttons with me in his carry case because I didn't want him getting lonely at home by himself. We hadn't managed to get very far in the rehearsal because Lucas and the director were having a row – AGAIN. Left the room, shouting at each other, they did. *Not* very professional, if you ask me." She rolled her eyes before carrying on, "And then the fire alarm started going off. Well, we didn't think much of it, to be honest, until suddenly the smoke started pouring in. Then those two teachers from the school burst through the doors and started shouting at everyone to get out. Marvellous, they were; such a nice pair." She smiled mistily and I felt my face pucker like I had eaten a sour lemon. *Nice* wasn't quite the word I would use for Miss Susan. Penny's smile disappeared as she carried on with her story, and tears filled her eyes. "But I couldn't find the carry case with Buttons in it. It was the most terrible, terrible thing. I was desperate, but the smoke was so thick and someone started pulling me out. I tried to get back in but the firefighter was holding me back. I can't understand how on earth Buttons got up there on the clock tower. He must have got out of the case somehow. . ." Penny drifted off, a puzzled look on her face before snapping back to attention. "Anyway, thank heavens he did or he would have been burnt to a crisp, and thank heavens for you, too, coming to the rescue!" She beamed at me.

"You said that Lucas and the director were fighting?" Ingrid asked thoughtfully. "Why was that?"

Magda and Penny shared a look. "Oh, you know

these 'big stars'," Magda said, putting little air quotes around the words with her fingers. "Everything's a HUGE drama, and to be honest, I don't think Lucas felt the part he was given was big enough. He's playing Macduff's son, so he only has a couple of lines."

I wanted to ask more questions, but I was interrupted by Derek Dweebles. His green checked suit was even more eye-watering up close and he brought with him the thick smell of cigar smoke.

"Ladies!" he boomed, smirking at Penny and Magda. "You're looking lovely this evening." He patted Penny on the arm. "I myself am thoroughly enjoying treading the boards." He turned his attention to all of us and waggled his eyebrows before making a little bow. "I'm playing the part of King Duncan, you know. Always thought I had a touch of royalty about me!" He honked with laughter then rubbed his hands together. "Hopefully we'll be able to raise plenty of cash, eh? So good of you all to volunteer for such a worthy cause. In fact, as proprietor of Dweebles's Cars, Brimwell's number one dealer in slightly used luxury automobiles, I have decided not only to offer my services as an actor, but to match all the money raised by the performance to rebuild the town hall." He raised a hand to silence Penny and Magda's exclamations. "No, no, say no more about it. We must all do our bit, after all," and he winked before continuing, "Speaking of which, where's our illustrious director, eh? The show must go on and all that. Time for us to get started." Without waiting for an answer he had swept through to the great hall and began giving the same speech to another group in there.

"Well," said Penny, her mouth slightly pursed as we followed Derek Dweebles into the hall. "I must say that was rather unexpected."

"You'd think he'd be the last to support any effort to rebuild the town hall!" Magda exclaimed and Penny nodded.

"Why's that?" I asked, puzzled.

"Oh, his car dealership is next door. He's been wanting to expand for ages, but he couldn't get planning permission so close to a historic site," Penny said. "I wonder what's in it for him? I've never known Derek Dweebles do anything out of the goodness of his heart."

"That's funny then," I said quickly. "Was he there too? You know, at the rehearsal when the fire started?"

Penny frowned. "Well, now that you mention it, he was supposed to be there for the rehearsal, but I don't remember him being there when the fire started. Probably off smoking one of his nasty cigars. . ."

But this insight into the character of Derek Dweebles came to an abrupt end as a thick silence filled the room. Standing in the doorway was a silver haired man in a long black cloak. He had one hand clutched tightly to his chest – and in the other glimmered a long silver dagger, dripping with blood.

CHAPTER TWELVE

The man stood in the doorway, a wild look in his dark, flashing eyes. He paused for a moment and then spoke.

"Is this a dagger which I see before me, the handle toward my hand? COME, LET ME CLUTCH THEE!" He thrust out his arm. The dagger got caught up in his cloak and there was a loud ripping sound. Ignoring this, the man threw the dagger to the ground with a clatter and fell to his knees. "OUT, OUT, BRIEF CANDLE!" he yelled, and then clutched at his chest again, gurgling loudly and writhing on the floor, until, after what felt like quite a long time, he gave one last enormous moan and lay still.

There was a long pause but finally someone

started clapping. Letty stepped forward, her face shining. "Bravo!" she shouted, and others joined in her applause. "Now *that's* what I call acting!" I heard Letty crow to the girl next to her.

"WHO..." asked Kip, his face scrunched in an expression of disgust generally saved for when he was told there was no pudding, "is THAT?!"

"Ooh, don't you know?" Penny giggled girlishly. "It's Maxwell Dangerfield, the director."

"What a hunk!" said Magda in a moony voice. "He used to play Hector Fink-Barton in *All Tomorrow's Yesterdays* until his character was thrown out of a window by his evil, blind, long-lost half-cousin, Maurice." She sighed. "Show business can be so fickle. If you ask me, *he's* the real star here. Still, at least he's found a second career as a director."

Maxwell Dangerfield had struggled to his feet and was bowing to the appreciative audience "Thank you, thank you," he intoned in a voice as slippery as a banana peel. "It is a thrill to be here, on this creative journey with all of you. I so admire your dedication to the craft, particularly after the tragedy of the recent fire, and I look forward to continuing our work on the Scottish Play in this new theatre." He beamed around at the crowd.

"The Scottish Play? Isn't that what Magda was going on about earlier?" Kip's loud voice echoed around the room. "I thought we were doing *Macbeth*?" Several people gasped and Maxwell Dangerfield clutched his chest so hard that I was worried that he was going to pretend to die again. "What did I say?" asked Kip, confused. "Macbeth? Aren't we doing *Macbeth*? That's what it says here on front of the *Macbeth* script. See? MACBETH."

The crowd of people were flinching and Ingrid had her hand pressed to her head.

"Stop saying that word!" she whispered.

"What word?" Kip was baffled, and so was I.

"THE M WORD!" Letty yelled.

"What? Macbeth?" Kip asked, bemused.

A hiss escaped from Maxwell Dangerfield. "My young friend!" he cried, pointing an accusing finger at Kip. "Can it be possible that you do not know about the *Scottish curse*?!"

Kip paled at that. "A c-c-curse?" he stuttered. "What is it with us and curses?!"

Kip certainly had a point there; after all it hadn't been long since we had been face to face with a seriously spooky ancient Egyptian curse. (If you want to know more about that I actually wrote a whole book about it, and if I wasn't being so polite and modest I would say it was maybe the *greatest book of our time*, so you might want to check it out.) I felt a chill spreading through me that was probably only partly related to the fact I had left my jumper back in the dorms. Curses, I knew, meant trouble.

Ingrid, however, was nodding. "It's a famous superstition in the theatre," she said, "I'm surprised you haven't heard of it."

"Superstition?!" snapped Maxwell. "It is no such thing. There is *documented evidence* of the Scottish curse. Everybody knows that speaking the name of this play while inside the theatre – unless you are reading from the actual script itself – spells disaster for the production." He paused ominously. "And we *certainly* don't need any more of that, do we?" The crowd murmured in agreement at this.

"I heard," chimed in Letty gleefully, "that the curse began because Shakespeare borrowed lines for the characters of the three witches from an actual coven of witches – and when they found out they were so angry they jinxed all future performances, and any actor who took part." A shudder ran through the room.

"Do you hear that?" cried Maxwell, "a jinx, young man, a jinx!"

"S-sorry," stammered Kip.

"And *I* heard," broke in Lucas Quest, "that at the very first performance of the play the prop dagger got swapped for a real dagger and the man playing King Duncan was *actually killed*." Everyone looked uneasily at the dagger lying on the ground by Maxwell's feet and over at Derek Dweebles, who wasn't looking as if the role of King Duncan was such a dream come true any more.

"And," continued Lucas, "in 1937 the tip came off one of the prop swords during the performance, flew into the audience and hit a man who had a heart attack." Lucas put his hand to his own chest before continuing. "In 1942 three actors in the production DIED . . . I could go on, the list is *endless*."

"You see!" Maxwell exclaimed. "This production has already had a bad start thanks to the fire and we certainly don't need any more accidents. You must perform the cleansing rituals."

"Cleansing rituals?" Kip repeated, a worried frown puckering his forehead. "What are those?"

"You must go outside, spin around three times and spit over your left shoulder," said Maxwell authoritatively.

"And then hop on your right leg for thirty seconds while clapping your hands and singing 'Twinkle Twinkle Little Star'," added Letty. "Otherwise, the ghosts of the witches will come and haunt us."

Kip looked torn between disbelief and fear, but seeing all the solemn faces around him he stomped off out of the door without another word. Through the open window we heard a loud and tuneless version of "Twinkle Twinkle Little Star" and eventually Kip stomped back in again. "Happy now?!" he muttered, folding his arms sulkily across his chest.

"Wonderful!" Maxwell sang out, radiant once more. "Now, open the curtains and let's get on this stage – it's time to begin the rehearsal!" With a flourish he tugged on the rope that pulled back the heavy red drapes.

A collective gasp knocked the air out of all of us, and someone let out a small scream of terror.

A large white sheet was hanging above the stage and on it, in jagged, dripping red letters was written:

SOMETHING WICKED THIS WAY COMES...

CHAPTER THIRTEEN

"What's that? Is that a line from *Macbeth*?" Kip's loud voice broke the horrified silence. Several furious faces turned in his direction. "Oh," he said sheepishly, "I said Macbeth again, didn't I?" He jumped. "Oops! And again. I'll just ... er ... run outside, shall I?" He plastered on a winning smile and disappeared from the room as fast as his quite short legs would carry him.

"Who is responsible for this ... this ... *outrage*?" Maxwell Dangerfield spun around to face the room. "Is this supposed to be some kind of joke?" Nobody said anything. Everyone looked too shocked.

Finally a shrill voice echoed through the room. "I've had just about all I can take of this!" a tiny, bird-like lady screeched in a trembly voice. "First the fire and now this? I'm sorry, but I can't stay here any longer. I'm just a bag of nerves. I'm starting to think this play really *is* jinxed! Come on, Martin," and she tugged at the arm of the very broad man standing next to her. "Let's go home." Martin shrugged his big shoulders and the two of them left together.

Maxwell groaned and he pressed his hand to his forehead. "Well, that is just wonderful!" he exclaimed with a stamp of his foot. "That's one of the three witches and our Banquo gone!" He threw his arms in the air. "Where could I find someone who knows the part at such short notice?"

"Ahem." Lucas Quest coughed delicately. "I don't know if you think I'd be right – but I do know the part," he said quietly. "And I'm very happy to take it on. If it will be helpful, I mean?" he added modestly, his eyes turned down towards the floor and a slight blush spreading across his cheeks. "After all," he said, looking up at Maxwell, "the part of Macduff's son that I am playing at the moment only has one small scene. I could do both – the audience wouldn't notice."

"Why, my dear boy, I think you're a trifle

young—" Maxwell began but he was swiftly shouted down by Derek Dweebles.

"Seems to me that beggars can't be choosers, Maxie. Especially if we are really facing some kind of jinx that's bumping us all off one by one!" He laughed loudly at that but several other cast members flinched. Seeing that his joke wasn't going down as well as he had expected, Dweebles's tone became more serious. "Plus the press will eat it up," he added. "After all the fire business Lucas is quite the local hero. Can't you just stick him in a false beard or something?"

"We-ell. . ." Maxwell looked torn.

"Only if the director thinks it is appropriate, of course," Lucas said gently. "If you think I can be of any help then I will do whatever I can. And I do know all the lines. . ." He threw back his head and let out a cry. "O, treachery! Fly, good Fleance, fly, fly, fly! Thou mayst revenge!" He lifted an arm as if to grasp something and then let it fall back to his side. A murmur of appreciation ran around the room.

"Yes, well, OK," Maxwell spluttered, looking around at the expectant faces. "I suppose the show must go on." But he looked a bit put out.

"I'll do the best I can," Lucas said, meekly.

Meanwhile, Letty had tentatively been taking down the gory sheet from across the stage. She examined it and wrinkled her nose. "It's just paint," she said. "And it's still wet."

"A foolish prank," said Maxwell firmly. "And in VERY bad taste. We've had enough distractions. Let's get this rehearsal moving."

"We'd better go and look for these props," Ingrid said, giving me a significant glance.

"Yes," I said loudly. "The props." We scuttled out of the great hall and through the entrance hall until we reached Kip, who was still hopping up and down outside.

"I think you can stop that now." Ingrid giggled.

"I don't think you can be too careful with a curse around," said Kip. "You know what happened last time."

"No," said Ingrid. "This time is totally different. It's just a silly superstition. After all, actors are a very superstitious bunch. You just have to humour them."

Kip didn't look convinced. "Yeah, well that might be more believable if there hadn't just been a terrible warning written in blood found on the stage," he said grumpily. "*And* this play has ghosts! AND it's about to be Halloween, which is only the SPOOKIEST time of the WHOLE YEAR." Kip was getting louder and louder. "Who's to say it wasn't because of this curse that the town hall burnt down?!"

"For starters," Ingrid said, raising a finger, "it wasn't blood, it was red paint. Doesn't seem like the undead to use poster paint, does it?"

"And," I jumped in, "thanks to Penny Farthing I would say we have a really good suspect for who could have started that fire. A HUMAN suspect," I added with a grin.

"Do we?" Kip looked surprised. "Who?"

"Derek Dweebles, of course!" I cried. "Magda and Penny seemed to think he was a sneaky character, up to no good, *and* they said that the town hall was in the way of him expanding his car dealership. He's a perfect suspect. Plus, Penny said he had mysteriously disappeared from the rehearsal, AND it was to smoke a cigar. SMOKE . . . FIRE . . . need I say more?!"

"Maybe," said Ingrid, thinking this over, "but he said he was going to match the money raised by the performance. Why would he burn down the town hall and then donate money to rebuild it?"

"I don't know," I admitted, "but there's definitely something suspicious about him."

110

Kip nodded. "He's a sneaky character. But what about that message in there? *Something wicked this way comes . . .* what's that all about?"

"Maxwell seems to think it was just a prank," Ingrid said.

"Well, it's a bit of a coincidence if you ask me," said Kip. "First the fire and then the warning? Someone or SOMETHING doesn't want the play to go ahead."

"But that's it!" I exclaimed. "If the play *doesn't* go ahead then Dweebles doesn't have to pay a penny, does he? Maybe he's just trying to throw suspicion off himself. After all, if he offers to donate money to the town hall fund no one will think he had anything to do with it."

I was feeling very pleased with myself! It was a great theory and I could tell Kip and Ingrid were impressed. Still, at the moment it was only a theory and we were going to need a lot more evidence to back it up. It was time to get investigating.

CHAPTER FOURTEEN

Unfortunately, we were so busy trying to track down all of the props on Letty's list that we didn't manage to do any more detecting that evening. The rest of the rehearsal went smoothly, and I had to admit that Lucas Quest was quite good as Banquo, even if he did look a bit silly all wrapped up in his winter get-up. When Maxwell asked him if he might like to take off his coat, Lucas shivered and said he was just worried about losing his voice and letting everyone down.

When they were rehearsing a scene he wasn't in, I was surprised to look up and find Lucas standing next to me as I sorted through a box of prop helmets. I gave him a small smile, and in return earned a grin so dazzling it made me feel like I needed a pair of sunglasses. "Hi," said Lucas Quest, giving a little self-conscious laugh. "I saw you looking at me; you must be a member of the QFF? Always nice to meet a fan!"

I snorted, then seeing that he was serious I said, "Er– no, actually. I'm not a member, sorry."

Lucas's smile dimmed a little. "But you've seen *Love Vampire: Vampire in Love*." It seemed like it should be a question but he said it as if he was just saying a fact about me like, "Your eyes are green."

"Nope," I said lightly. "It's not really my kind of thing, to be honest."

"Oh." Lucas floundered. "There's going to be another one you know," he blurted. "A Love Vampire sequel. And my part's much bigger this time."

"Oh, right," I said. "Well, that's nice for you. . ." Neither of us were sure what to say next so we stood in uncomfortable silence for a moment. "Well, I'd better get back to this," I said gesturing towards the box in front of me.

"Right, yes," Lucas said. "Er. . . bye then." He wandered off, his gloved hands stuffed in his coat pockets, until a pair of girls I didn't know wearing purple QFF badges fluttered over to him, and the

113

toothpaste-advert-worthy smile came out again. I shook my head. *What a strange boy.*

After the rehearsal had finished and everyone had left, Ingrid, Kip and I tidied the props and mooched through the hall. In one of the post cubbyholes that covered the far wall I spied an envelope sticking out above the gold plaque with my name on it. I rushed over to it and felt my heart grow a bit inside my chest as I recognized the writing as Pym's. "Yes!" I waved the envelope in the air. "A letter from the circus!"

"Oh, lucky you—" Kip began, but just then we were distracted by a sudden crash coming from somewhere above on the grand stone staircase that ran up the middle of the main building.

"Is somebody there?" I called, climbing the stairs with Kip and Ingrid hot on my heels. "Are you all right?"

As we rounded the first bend in the staircase we came upon a very red-faced Maxwell Dangerfield, wrestling with a large oil portrait which had clearly been hanging on the wall.

"Ah, children!" he cried. "I wonder if you could give me some assistance." We hurried over and between us managed to hang the enormous picture back on the wall.

"Thank you," he panted when we were done, and he pulled out a handkerchief with which he wiped his glowing face. "I was just admiring this painting here when I realized that it would be perfect for hanging in one of the interior sets for the play. I'm afraid I got rather carried away and took it down to have a better look, but then I couldn't get it back up. What a blessing that you were still around – I thought everyone had gone home." He gave us a very toothy smile.

I looked at the painting. It was one of many that crowded the walls lining the staircase, and I must have walked past it a hundred times without ever noticing it before. It was a pretty gloomy portrait of a serious-looking man with a neat grey beard. He was dressed all in black including his top hat, and carrying a cane, the handle of which was shaped like a duck's head. You could tell that the building behind him was Saint Smithen's.

Kip had his head cocked to one side and he was staring very hard at the portrait.

"What's wrong, Kip?" I asked.

Kip paused before speaking, looking very serious. "Do you think ... that top hat makes him look taller?" he asked.

I groaned and Ingrid looked like she was trying not to laugh.

Maxwell Dangerfield looked confused. "Taller?" he echoed.

"Yes," Kip nodded. "You may not have noticed so much, because I recently grew one eighth of an inch thanks to an increase in my sprout consumption, but I am actually *very slightly* vertically challenged."

Maxwell cleared his throat. "Ah," he murmured, obviously not sure how to respond.

Kip nodded again. "You're right. I think the hat would look great on me."

Maxwell seemed to have recovered by now. "Perhaps you could ask Magda if we have one in the costume department?" he said smoothly, with another charming smile.

"Great idea, thanks!" said Kip, looking thrilled.

With that we all walked back down the stairs and Maxwell bid us goodnight.

"I look forward to another rehearsal on Thursday" he said, and after he had left we said goodnight to Kip, and Ingrid and I headed back to our room.

When I was settled into bed and Ingrid was happily reading, I tore open the envelope containing the letter from my family.

Dear Poppy,

I'm so sorry that our phone call was cut short. You'll be pleased to hear that we are all friends again now. Marvin apologized to Leaky Sue for disappearing her, Leaky Sue apologized for insulting Luigi's moustache, and Luigi apologized for feeding her hat to Buttercup. At that point there were some minor setbacks because it would seem that Leaky Sue had, until then, been ignorant of this fact. Fortunately everyone came out reasonably unscathed and Luigi's moustache is already growing back in nicely. Anyway, we're all looking forward to seeing you for Parents' Weekend and catching up with all your news.

Lots of love,

Pym XXX

Poppers,

Just wanted to add a note to say that I disagree in the <u>strongest possible terms</u> with Pym's description of us all as "friends". I have been horrifically disfigured and my honour has been insulted. I shall never again be able to look a lampshade in the eye. My little Buttercup has been horribly sick. Forgive the ink blots... she has also been chewing my pen.

I remain your most humble and devoted servant.

Luigi

Hi Poppy,

We wanted to say hello. And also to tell you that we really enjoyed the book on famous twins that you got for our birthday. It was

BAH! TOMATO! IT IS TAKING TOO LONG FOR MY TURN. BUTTERCUP IS BEEN SICK IN MARVIN'S HAT. HE IS SO CROSS THAT HE LOOK LIKE TOMATO AS WELL! IS HILARIOUS. LEAKY SUE SAYS IT IS HIS JUST DESSERTS BUT I DO NOT UNDERSTAND THIS EXPRESSION. I HOPE SHE WILL NOT MAKE HIM EAT THE LION SICK. THAT IS DISGUSTING.

FANELLA

By the end of the letter I was spluttering with giggles and I could barely breathe. Letty and Ingrid wanted to know what on earth was going on so I read them the letter and we all ended up laughing so loudly that there was a sharp knock at the door. I gulped and swallowed my mirth as quickly as I could.

Miss Susan's face appeared, looking just as cross as it usually did when it was looking in my direction. "Why am I not surprised to find all this racket is coming from your room, Poppy?"

"Sorry, miss," I said. But something terrible was happening. All those laughs that I had stuffed down and swallowed when Miss Susan knocked on the door were shaking inside me like wriggly, wobbly jelly. I couldn't look Ingrid and Letty in the eye, but from the way their shoulders were shaking it looked as if they were having the same problem.

"It's time you had the lights off and were all asleep," Miss Susan was saying. "I could hear your commotion from all the way down the hall."

"S-s-sorry, miss," I gasped again, my voice wobbling dangerously.

Miss Susan gave me a piercing glare and without any further ado she switched off the light and shut the door behind her. I buried my face in my pillow and muffled all the laughter that spilled out of me. Just when I had calmed down Letty's voice whispered through the dark – "Lion sick!" – and the three of us dissolved into nearly silent giggles once more.

CHAPTER FIFTEEN

We met Kip in the dining hall for breakfast the next morning. I have to admit I still found it tough to hide my disappointment at the bowls of soggy cornflakes on offer after a lifetime spent chomping popcorn and marshmallow sprinkles for breakfast. (Ingrid says I'm a medical miracle and that one day dentists will line up to study me and work out why all my teeth haven't fallen out.) After I had gulped down a few mushy spoonfuls it was time for the three of us to push off to lessons. That's the trouble with school, you know. There always seem to be lessons to get to, even when you have got a mystery to solve.

First up we had a history lesson with Professor Tweep, who had us in tears as he enacted the final moments of Marie Antoinette before she was led to the guillotine. For a man who looks a bit like a bespectacled walrus he made a surprisingly convincing French queen.

"You should join the Brimwell players, sir," I said admiringly.

Professor Tweep puffed up a bit at that. "Very kind, Miss Pym," he said. "Might have to look in on a rehearsal, eh? Now, back to Marie Antoinette—"

Kip's arm shot up in the air so fast I thought he was going to dislocate his shoulder.

"She's the one that said, 'Let them eat cake,'" he said, squirming in his seat. "I think that shows top royal skills, making sure everyone had a nice piece of cake. I wish more people made cake a priority. If I were the king I'd say, 'Let them eat cake, AND biscuits, AND donuts, AND—'"

Professor Tweep cleared his throat. "Well, that's not precisely what it means..." he began, when Ingrid, who had been staring absently at the ceiling, broke in, dreamy and half-asleep.

"And actually, it's extremely unlikely Marie Antoinette ever said that at all. The quote is popularly attributed to Rousseau who wrote it years earlier."

"Quite right, Miss Blammel," Professor Tweep wheezed, a smile spreading across his face like butter across a scone.

Kip's face fell. "No . . . cake?" he asked.

"No cake," the professor confirmed.

Kip sighed, muttered, "Another moment in cake history utterly ruined," and sank his head into his hands.

"Now. Imagine Marie Antoinette's anguish in 1793 when spending her final three months in a prison cell, separated from her children," Professor Tweep continued. "And how frightened and alone they must have been! Can you imagine being separated from your own mother in such a way? Her daughter was only fifteen at the time . . . not much older than you are now. Imagine how you would feel – not being able to see or talk to your mother, not even knowing whether she was dead or alive."

The room was quiet, but my heart was not. In fact, I was surprised that no one was turning around to see who it was that had swallowed a massive, noisy drum as it hammered away in my chest.

Of course this wasn't the first time that someone had mentioned mothers in front of me. Until you don't have one I don't suppose you notice how much they come up in everyday life. Still, it felt like something in Professor Tweep's words touched on a problem that was really bothering me, and as he continued with the lesson I couldn't stop thinking about it. I had been separated from my mother for eleven years. Who was she? Where was she? And was SHE thinking about ME?

After lessons had finished I knew I had to finally turn my attention to Miss Baxter's school history assignment. (I bet you had forgotten about that. That's the trouble with being a top class detective when you're eleven. There's always homework getting in the way.) Between our investigation into the fire and the play I hadn't even had time to think about it, but now I quite liked the idea of some time to myself to mull everything over in between learning facts about Saint Smithens. "I'll meet you in the dining hall for dinner," I told Kip and Ingrid, slipping out into the cool, clear evening air and making my way towards the reassuring calm of the library.

Mr Fipps the librarian was asleep when I got there. I coughed gently and he awoke with a loud spluttering and peered at me over the top of his round spectacles.

"History of the school, eh?" he muttered, when I had repeated my assignment three times. "Better follow me."

He led the way, winding through the library stacks in a determined march. "Ahh. Here we are." He paused in front of a bookcase. "Local history, sub-section: Saint Smithen's. Some crackers in here." He began tugging books off the shelf and piling them up in my arms until I was swaying beneath their weight. "That should be enough to get you started, but if you have any questions, or if you need more help, make sure you come back and see me." His eyes were sparkling now and he seemed wide awake. It was obvious how much he loved the library, and I gave him a big blazing smile, hoping that he would recognize a kindred spirit.

I spent some time flipping through a couple of books but found it difficult to focus. I couldn't stop thinking about Marie Antoinette and her daughter being separated and neither one knowing if the other was all right. I wondered if somewhere out there was a lady who looked a bit like me, worrying about her daughter. With a sigh I gave up trying to read and gathered everything together into my backpack. I staggered back to the dining hall, bending under the weight, just in time to join Kip and Ingrid at the dining table.

Kip pointed to my bulging backpack as I dropped it down beside my chair. "What's in there? Rocks?"

"Feels like it. I've just broken my back lugging all of those over from the library. I'm not exactly strongman material yet. It's books."

These were the magic words as far as Ingrid was concerned, and she tore into my school bag as if it were a fat, shining present on Christmas morning. "Oh yes, *The Complete History of Saint Smithen's* by Letitia Blackstone is absolutely KEY; such a great book," she said with a nod as she carefully unpacked the books on to the table. "And *Saint Smithen: The Man Behind the Miracles* is a classic. She paused as she pulled out a slim paperback with a faded green cover. "What's this?" she said, gently fluttering the pages. "I've never seen it before." She looked closely at the faint writing on the cover. "*The Secret History of Phineas Scrimshaw*," she read.

"Phineas Scrimshaw?" repeated Kip, taking a break from shovelling his dinner into his mouth. "What sort of a name is that?"

"Who is he?" I asked.

Ingrid was leafing through the pages. "He was

the last owner of Saint Smithen's before it became a school, over a hundred and fifty years ago. I thought everyone knew that!"

Kip and I exchanged a look. "Oh yeah," said Kip sarcastically. "EVERYONE knows that."

Ingrid nodded eagerly, her eyes rapidly scanning the pages in front of her. "But I didn't know any of this. This is fascinating," she added.

"Yeah, I bet," I mumbled. Ingrid and I often have quite different ideas about what is fascinating and what is not.

"Listen to this!" Ingrid exclaimed, ignoring us. "Phineas Scrimshaw was a notorious miser and his vast fortune has never been recovered."

"Miser?" I frowned. I wasn't quite sure what that meant.

"Fortune?" said Kip through a mouthful of mashed potatoes.

"Yes. A miser is someone who hoards all their money and never likes to spend any of it," Ingrid said thoughtfully. "And, according to this book, Phineas Scrimshaw hid all of his gold and it was never found."

"Never found?" I echoed, my voice sounding like it was coming from somewhere far away.

Kip swallowed his potatoes. "You mean like . . . buried treasure?!" Excitement fizzed up in his voice like the bubbles in a can of cherry cola.

"Yes," said Ingrid briskly. "Exactly like buried treasure. Millions of pounds worth of gold to be precise."

I could hear my heart beating in my ears. The man who used to live in this school, in the very building we were *sitting* in, had buried a hidden fortune somewhere. Was it possible that we had just stumbled on to our next mystery? *Another* mystery? A mystery that came complete with a hoard of buried gold?! Were my dreams of becoming a top detective coming true once more? My stomach rumbled with excitement. (And possibly a bit of hunger.)

"So you're saying," I said slowly, trying to keep my voice steady, "that no one ever found Phineas Scrimshaw's treasure? This book says it is still out there somewhere, just waiting to be discovered?"

"No. Not *out there*," Ingrid said, her eyes meeting mine. "Right here. His treasure is buried somewhere at Saint Smithen's."

CHAPTER SIXTEEN

The three of us sat staring at each other. *Buried treasure! Somewhere here at Saint Smithen's!* I felt a fizzing glow spread through my body, leaving me crackling like a frayed wire. "What do you mean, *here at Saint Smithen's?*" I asked breathlessly. "What does it say?"

Kip's head was swinging around on his neck and he peered around the dining room as if expecting a massive hoard of gold to appear at any moment.

Ingrid's forehead crinkled. "I'm not sure," she admitted. "It's pretty strange. This is what it says: *The legend of Scrimshaw's gold is well known to the reader, but the clues needed to unlock the miser's riddle remain, as yet, undiscovered. Rumour has it that the gold* is hidden somewhere in the grounds of Saint Smithen's itself, and while this seems likely, the author has been unable to obtain verification for himself." Ingrid stopped reading and looked up. "It's funny, but someone has underlined all these bits about the treasure. And with a green pen as well. I hate that! You shouldn't write in a library book," she finished crossly. But I wasn't going to be distracted from the new information Ingrid had revealed.

"Who wrote this book?" I asked.

Ingrid turned to the front of the slender volume in her hands. "It's by someone called Edward Ashby-Gordon... Gosh!" she exclaimed. "And this edition is almost a hundred years old." Well, that makes scribbling in it even more criminal," she huffed, with a frown.

Kip interrupted us. "But hang on a second. If that book is so old, all the gold could have already been found years and years ago." He looked a bit grumpy at the thought of someone else finding all the gold that he had already decided was rightfully his.

"No." Ingrid shook her head. "If someone had found a hoard of buried gold at Saint Smithen's then it would definitely be mentioned in one of the books I've read about this place. In fact, the only reason I haven't heard of any of this before must be because it's probably just a rumour."

"You don't know that!" Kip jumped up. "For all you know there's a secret chamber full of gold under your feet right this second!"

I was still staring at the book. "And what's all this about riddles and clues?" I asked. Then, feeling like a world-class detective, I said solemnly, "There's more to this story than meets the eye."

"Another mystery!" shouted Kip.

"Another mystery indeed," I said, tapping my nose with a knowing look.

Ingrid still looked a bit doubtful. "I'm not sure we need another mystery when we are already working on one," she said. "Plus, how do we know any of this is even true?"

"Well, there's one way to find out." I said with a grin, "it's back to the library after dinner!"

"Back so soon, Poppy?" said Mr Fipps as we pushed through the swing doors and marched up to his desk. He had half a cheese sandwich in one hand, and a steaming thermos sat on the desk beside him.

"Sorry to interrupt your dinner, Mr Fipps," I said briskly. "But we have a research-based emergency."

His eyes lit up and the sandwich dropped from his hand. He wiped his fingers on a red spotted handkerchief and pushed his spectacles up his nose. "How can I be of assistance?" he asked.

"Our current research has left us with some questions," said Ingrid, taking out the Phineas Scrimshaw book, opening it to the right page, and handing it to Mr Fipps. "We're interested to find out more about what the author calls 'the legend of Scrimshaw's gold'. Can you help us?" She pointed to the passage in the book and Mr Fipps read it carefully.

"*Rumour has it that the gold is hidden somewhere in the grounds of Saint Smithen's itself* . . . Interesting," he said softly. He flipped to the front of the book.

"And someone's *written* in it!" huffed Ingrid, her eyes wide behind her glasses.

"Yes, don't you just hate that?" said Mr Fipps. "Although in this case I believe the damage was done *before* it became a library book. I think this book was part of a donation to the library from a local family a few years ago, and I seem to remember it being in a fairly poor condition. Still, it's a difficult book to find and beggars can't be choosers." He smiled, and flicked through the book. "I see it was published in 1907." He tapped a finger to his chin thoughtfully. "Well, the author seems to think the story was quite well known at the time. Shouldn't be too difficult to track something down in the relevant archives. You'd better wait here."

He disappeared into the small room behind his desk. The sign on the door that he left slightly ajar read: RECORDS.

The three of us stood in silence, holding our breath and hoping that our potential mystery wouldn't hit a dead end straight away. After what felt like hours we heard Mr Fipps's voice drift through. "Ah!" he sighed, happily. "Got you." Then we heard the sound of the photocopier whirring to life and soon he emerged.

"I think you'll find this particular diary very interesting. This should shed some light on the matter," he said, handing us the still-warm pages and standing back with his hands on his hips like a triumphant librarian superhero.

"Thank you very much," I squeaked, looking at the pieces of paper in my hands. They were photocopied pages from an old journal or diary and I felt my excitement rising again. One look at the first words written there was enough to convince me that we really did have another case to crack.

CHAPTER SEVENTEEN

<u>4th September 1848</u>

It has been almost twenty-five years since the death of my father and yet our hunt for his hidden fortune continues. There are a mere three days remaining before our poverty forces through the sale of the family estate and it becomes a preparatory school for boys. The humiliation! The degradation! How shall we, the honourable Scrimshaws, hold our heads high in this wretched community? We have launched another thorough search of the house and grounds but I fear that like all the rest this too shall prove fruitless. Curse my selfish Papa! Or should I begin to call him "Old

Skinflint Scrimshaw", as the locals do? Why must he continue to torment us in this way? Where has he hidden the Scrimshaw gold?

5th September 1848

As predicted the current search has thus far proved a dead end. It is well known throughout the county that during his lifetime, Papa was a notorious penny-pincher. He used to eat only the cheapest cuts of meat, wear only the shabbiest clothes, and allowed our once glorious home to fall into a state of disrepair. And yet we know that the Scrimshaw fortune was vast. Not that we ever saw any of it. The old man would never so much as settle a single one of my debts, and, after all, a young man in the prime of his life is sure to get a little behind with his payments every now and then. You make one small mistake like betting some of your inheritance on a bad horse and suddenly you're "financially useless".

6th September 1848

It has come to this, then – our beloved Scrimshaw Hall to be sold off, and our once glorious family name in tatters. My father continues to torment us from beyond the grave with his riddles. If anyone should, by chance, stumble upon this diary in future years perhaps they shall have better luck than we wretched creatures with his fiendish treasure hunt. Dear reader, upon opening my father's will these twenty-five years past we found not the loving wishes of a devoted father, but the cruel game of a true miser. Here then I lay out the first clue in its entirety, and I wish you joy of it.

Riddle me one, the first of three

That must be solved to find the key.

If gold you seek, or precious stones,

Then set a fire beneath my bones.

Can anyone solve this riddle? And with the sale of our family home, and the gold still missing, is the miser's revenge finally complete? I feel as though there is a jinx upon us all and I despair.

A stunned silence filled the air as we finished reading, squished up in a corner of the library. "His bones?!" Kip exclaimed, breaking the stillness. "He wants people to set fire to his bones? That is seriously creepy. Where are his bones anyway?"

"In the graveyard at Saint Smithen's church, I suppose," murmured Ingrid. "But that doesn't make much sense, does it? Even if you did have to burn up his bones, how could that possibly help?"

"Mr Fipps!" I called out as the librarian rushed past us with another worried-looking student in tow. "Sorry to bother you, but this is so interesting. Is there any more of this diary to read?"

"I'm afraid not, Miss Pym," he answered. "That's all we have in the records room. It's a wonder something like that has survived this long." He sighed blissfully. "That's the power of the library, you see!" and he scampered off to help another student in need.

"No wonder nobody has been able to solve it," I said with a frown. "It doesn't make a bit of sense. Why would Old Scrimshaw want to make it impossible for his son to inherit the money?"

"I don't know," Ingrid said reluctantly. "I think he

set up the clue just to torment his family – his son sounds pretty horrid. I don't think he cared about his father one bit – only his money. I'm not sure this is really worth investigating."

Kip jumped to his feet. "How can you say that, Ingrid?!" he exclaimed. "There could be mounds of hidden gold somewhere in the school and you don't want to look for it? Imagine what you could buy with all that gold. IMAGINE THE CAKE, INGRID. Endless cake. Cake as far as the eye can see!" Kip's eyes glazed over slightly as he disappeared into fantasies of cake mountains.

"I didn't say that I didn't want to look for it," Ingrid sighed, "but we already have a mystery to solve – or have you forgotten about Derek Dweebles? The play being sabotaged? The FIRE?!" Her voice got louder and louder as she ran through our admittedly quite long list of current investigations.

Kip threw his hands in the air. "What do you think, Poppy?" he asked.

I let out a low whistle. "I don't know," I said. "You wait your whole life for a good mystery and suddenly there are so many you can't keep track." I thought for a moment. "I don't think we should turn our backs on such a good case," I said finally. "That's not what a good detective does. As Dougie Valentine says: 'Follow the clues wherever they lead and you are certain to succeed, now outta my way, zombies!' Although," I added, "on reflection, that last bit probably isn't so relevant for us."

"OK." Ingrid nodded. "You're right. But how are we going to handle two cases? That's a lot of work."

Kip looked daunted. "Even for three ace detectives like us," he agreed.

"I know! We *can* do both!" I leapt to my feet in excitement. "Before we do anything else we need to learn more about this treasure hunt. What better place to start than by interviewing a bunch of people who've lived here all their lives? The Brimwell town players! We can carry on with our investigation of Dweebles and ask some questions about Phineas Scrimshaw at the same time."

"Poppy's right," said Ingrid. "If the stories about Scrimshaw's gold are true then surely someone in the Brimwell Players will have heard them."

"And they're all SO OLD!" Kip yelled enthusiastically. "They were probably all best mates with old Scrimshaw himself."

"Well, I don't think any of them are quite two

hundred years old just yet," I said, "but maybe they heard stories passed down from their great-grandparents or great-great-grandparents. You never know."

Kip looked at me admiringly. "Wow, Poppy! You're like a real detective!"

I tried to look modest but I could feel a big, unstoppable grin creeping all across my face. We had yet another mystery to solve and it was time for us to get to work.

CHAPTER EIGHTEEN

Luckily for our plan, the next rehearsal with the Brimwell players was the following day. The first clue was still rolling around in my head, but unfortunately there wasn't much time to daydream about discovering a lost fortune and buying a yacht and sailing around the world drinking cherry cola and eating bonbons when we had so much work to do. I felt so electrified by the mystery of it all that I was surprised sparks weren't shooting out of my fingers.

"We'll do questions about Phineas Scrimshaw first," I whispered, laying out our plan as we arrived at the rehearsal. "Just to see if there are any nibbles. Then we need to try and establish where Dweebles was during the fire. We have motive, now let's find out if he had opportunity."

"Who shall we speak to first?" whispered Ingrid. "Her?"

I sighed. I hadn't imagined us voluntarily approaching Penny Farthing for another conversation; still, I had to admit she had been a good source of information so far.

However, we didn't get a chance to ask Penny our well-rehearsed questions because she was already bursting with news of her own."Did you hear?" she blurted as we approached.

"Hear what?" I asked, confused.

"About the fire!" she exclaimed. Then, seeing the lack of comprehension on our faces, she added, "They're saying it definitely wasn't an accident! They're saying that someone started it deliberately!"

"Who is saying that?" I asked urgently.

"The police!" Penny said. "They came around to my house to interview me today – apparently they're interviewing everyone who was there." She looked torn between fear and excitement.

For the three of us this only confirmed our suspicions, but knowing that we had begun investigating the crime even before the police made me feel pretty important. "And that Inspector was a bit dishy!" Penny's giggles interrupted my thoughts.

"Inspector?" I echoed.

"Inspector Hartley. Didn't mind being interrogated by him, if you know what I mean!" she said with a wink.

I stifled a groan, not just because of what Penny had said, but because we had come across Inspector Arthur Hartley during our last case and I didn't think he was going to be too happy about us snooping around.

"I can't wait for Magda to get here," Penny continued. "We haven't had this much gossip in years!" She shook her head wonderingly. "I just can't believe anyone would burn down that amazing building on purpose. It is so sad. Two hundred years of history gone like that." she clicked her fingers.

"The town hall was two hundred years old?" asked Ingrid beadily. "What a coincidence," she continued airily, and I glanced at her in admiration. "We're doing a bit of a project on someone who was alive exactly then – Phineas Scrimshaw. Have you ever heard of him?" The three of us turned expectant eyes in Penny's direction.

"Well, of course I have," Penny laughed a flutey little laugh. "I'm his last remaining relative."

"What?!" Kip, Ingrid and I exclaimed in one big voice.

Penny giggled. "Oh yes, it's quite true. I am a direct descendent of Lord Scrimshaw, on my mother's side. Brimwell royalty, some people call me, but I don't like to draw attention to myself." She said this in a loud and important voice, which led me to believe she wasn't exactly being truthful on the attention-drawing front.

"Wow!" I said, clasping my hands and trying to look impressed. "That's amazing. We've been doing some research on Phineas Scrimshaw – for school, you know – and he seems like such an interesting character."

"Oh, he was," Penny puffed herself up a bit, "and he did so much for this community. After all, it was he who built the town hall in the first place."

Phineas Scrimshaw had built the town hall? That was news to us. How did that fit in with what we already knew? If anything, it seemed pretty out of character for a miser to spend lots of money on a building for other people. I felt in my bones that this was an important clue but for now I wasn't sure why. . .

"That's interesting," said Ingrid slowly as if she was reading my mind. "I thought he was a miser? Wouldn't it have been expensive to build a whole town hall?"

Penny sighed and shook her head. "People always remember him as this terrible miser of course, but that was only when he was much older. As a young man he did so much for Brimwell – building the town hall and establishing a museum there. And he spent a lot of money on this building. . ." she said, gesturing around the school hall where we stood. "Funny to think this was my ancestral home! And you've got Lord Scrimshaw to thank for this very room – all the original features here were his design. It's beautiful."

We all looked around the great hall and it felt like for the first time I was really noticing all the amazing details. I'd always thought it was very grand, but now I took in the blue and gilt design on the high ceiling, the enormous, ornate fireplace, and the elaborately carved wooden panelling on the walls, with their intricate pattern of leaves, flowers and woodland creatures. Saint Smithen's was so big and old that sometimes you took these things for granted but Penny was right: the room really was beautiful.

"But what about the treasure?!" burst out Kip, and Ingrid and I glared at him. We were trying to be subtle, after all.

Penny only laughed. "Oh, you've been reading that old story, have you? Well, I don't believe a word of it myself. I think the whole thing was just some big prank."

"What about the clue, though?" Kip persisted. "The one he left in his will about burning his bones?"

"All nonsense, I'm afraid." Penny shook her head. "Believe me, several generations of Scrimshaws spent their lives trying to get to the bottom of it. They turned that graveyard upside down. Apparently they even went through his coffin before he was laid to rest, which I think is a bit much. There was one lunatic later on who wanted to dig him up and burn his body, he took that clue so literally." A shiver ran down all our spines, as Penny continued. "I'm sorry to say it, but the whole thing's a hum. That clue makes no sense at all." She looked at our downcast faces, sympathetically. "But I do have some old family papers somewhere," she said. "Perhaps you would like to come for tea and have a look for your project?"

Kip and Ingrid's eyes lit up like dazzling spotlights shining on Penny's face and I'm sure mine must have looked exactly the same. Then a thought struck and I felt myself deflate.

"That's so kind, Penny, and we would love to, but I don't think Miss Baxter will let us go." I sighed. "We're not supposed to leave the school grounds without a teacher."

"You leave Miss Baxter to me," twinkled Penny. "After what you did for my Buttons I'm only sorry I didn't think of it sooner."

"Well, that would be amazing!" I cried, my enthusiasm tumbling over Kip and Ingrid's own agreements.

Penny looked pleased at our excitement, but our conversation was interrupted by the arrival of Miss Marigold. "Would anyone like a biscuit?" she asked, holding a plate of fat chocolate chip cookies in front of her. The smell was delicious and a whole crowd materialised around her, including all of us. (Kip was by her side before she had even finished her sentence. In fact, his nose had been sniffing the air like a bloodhound just before Miss Marigold walked through the door.)

"Do they have any peanuts in?" Penny asked.

"I'm deathly allergic, you see."

"No peanuts" said Miss Marigold cheerfully, then in a lower voice she continued, "and did you speak to that inspector today, Penny? What a turn up for the books!" The two women wandered off, gossiping, and leaving us to munch our still warm biscuits.

"Do you think Miss Baxter will let us go to Penny's?" Ingrid asked, watching Penny and Miss Marigold totter off.

"If she doesn't I expect Penny will just squish her in one of her death grips," muttered Kip, rubbing his neck.

"She certainly does like hugging people," I said, my attention drifting to our surroundings. I looked around at the jumble of Brimwell residents, teachers and students who filled the hall. Gary the plumber and star of the show was busy stuffing his face with sandwiches and chatting with Banquo, who was being played by Lucas Quest in a very bushy false beard that might have once been part of a Father Christmas costume. Then the sound of clapping hands drew everyone's attention as Maxwell Dangerfield stood onstage. The rehearsal was about to begin.

CHAPTER NINETEEN

Kip, Ingrid and I scuttled over to the side of the stage where we had carefully laid out the props.

Magda was there and she took her place on stage, holding a broomstick alongside another lady I didn't know, and Madame Patrice, who had been drafted in to play the role of the Third Witch after the original actor had stormed out of the last rehearsal.

"Here I have a pilot's thumb, wreck'd as homeward he did come," Magda cackled, and Maxwell pointed at Kip who started banging enthusiastically on a drum.

"A drum, a drum! Macbeth doth come," Madame Patrice cried, waving her arms from side to side. Then all three witches started chanting and

Madame Patrice began whirling across the stage. Letty pressed the button on the smoke machine and clouds of smoke began to billow across the ground.

Kip was bashing the drum with such determination that it was a bit difficult to hear what the witches were saying, but overall the effect was very spooky – I was impressed.

Now it was time for the characters of Macbeth and Banquo to enter the scene.

"So foul and fair a day I have not seen," Macbeth – or Gary – gasped, beads of sweat running down his face.

"Wow!" I whispered to Ingrid. "That's amazing acting. He really looks as though all this inner turmoil is making him ill."

"I think he actually is ill!" Ingrid whispered back. Now she mentioned it he did look quite green.

Lucas was talking now but Gary was swaying on the spot. Lucas finished his lines and looked at Gary. Gary looked back at Lucas. A heavy silence filled the air.

"Speak, if you can," someone hissed from behind the curtain.

"That's a bit mean," I muttered. "He's obviously forgotten his next line."

"'Speak, if you can' *is* his next line," said Ingrid, pointing to the script.

"Speak if you can," the voice hissed again, more urgently.

Gary opened his mouth. And was promptly sick all over Magda's shoes.

"Uggggh!" Magda cried, jumping back from the river of vomit that flowed in her direction, and teetering on the edge of the stage. I ran towards her but it was too late. Magda fell backwards with a tremendous crash. "Oooooooowww!" she howled. "My ankle!" Everything was in uproar.

Letty had leapt forward and was trying to put a screeching Magda into the recovery position. The lady playing the Second Witch had clamped her own hands over her mouth and fled off stage. Gary was now being sick into a prop helmet that Ingrid had handed him, and Madame Patrice was performing an elaborate tap dance at the front of the stage, shouting, "The show must go on! I've seen far worse than this in my time at the West End!"

Maxwell Dangerfield stood with his head in his hands, and Derek Dweebles burst through the door. "Sorry I'm late," he boomed. "Had to answer a lot of questions with that blinkin' police officer—" He stopped short, taking in the scene in front of him. "Blimey O'Reilly, what's going on here then?" he asked, dumbstruck.

It took about thirty minutes to get everything cleaned up and straightened out. Penny had taken Magda, a very pale Gary and a weeping Second Witch home in her car to recover. All three had made it clear that they wouldn't be coming back. It seemed as though a jinx really had struck this performance. Now we all stood around waiting to see what Maxwell Dangerfield was going to say. He was pacing up and down and muttering to himself.

I took this opportunity to sidle up to Derek Dweebles who was looking thoroughly miserable in his bright orange suit. "Tough day?" I asked, sympathetically.

Dweebles let out a big sigh. "You don't know the half of it," he said. "I spent two hours being interrogated by some jumped-up policeman about the town hall fire."

"Oh, really?" I asked innocently.

"Yes, and it was a bloomin' cheek!" he snapped. "They wanted to know to know if I had an alibi. Me! A respected pillar of the community. So I told them, I had sneaked out of the rehearsal to close a deal on a slightly used Ford Escort. I was at my dealership the whole time until I heard all the commotion outside, and there's security cameras and witnesses there that could tell them the same." He shook his head grumpily. "It's outrageous that a man of my calibre should be treated as a suspect. I mean, look at me... Do I look like a criminal to you?!"

I dutifully shook my head but my mind was reeling. Dweebles had an alibi?! But if that was true then our number one suspect, really our only suspect, was out of the picture.

"Truth be told," Dweebles continued in a low voice, "I've been thinking about running for mayor – trying to get some goodwill going with donating to the town hall fund. But if word gets out that I'm a suspect in an arson case then my chances will be scuppered." With a start he seemed to realize that he was saying all of this aloud. "So ... er ... keep it to yourself, if you don't mind, young lady!" His voice got very jolly and he patted me on the shoulder.

After muttering some sympathetic and agreeable-sounding mutterings I returned to Kip and Ingrid. "We need to talk!" I whispered, but then Maxwell Dangerfield clapped his hands and all eyes turned in his direction.

"Well, ladies and gentlemen, we have a problem. Not only are we two witches down, but we seem to have lost our leading man with three days to go before the performance. It appears to me that there is only one possible course of action. . ." He drifted off.

"Ahem." Lucas Quest cleared his throat. "Perhaps—"

Maxwell lifted his hand. "Yes. There is only one person who can step into the spotlight. The show must go on, and I, Maxwell Dangerfield, will be the star."

Lucas looked like someone had just slapped him in the face with a wet shoe. Everyone else started clapping. Maxwell lifted his hands again. "Although," his brow wrinkled, "this does leave us in the difficult position of being short several actors *and* a director. We need some new recruits and fast. Who can we get in at such short notice with excellent performing experience? We need people who are so fearless they won't be put off by this jinx nonsense."

There was a despair-soaked pause, and I cleared my throat. "Um . . . I think I might know some people who can help with that."

CHAPTER TWENTY

In the end it wasn't difficult to arrange for the circus to come – after all, it was only a day earlier than they were supposed to arrive for Parents' Weekend anyway and Miss Baxter gave them permission to set up camp in the school grounds. Fortunately they didn't have a performance scheduled (even circus troupes deserve a well-earned break every now and then), so Pym was only too happy to receive Miss Baxter's phone call.

Kip, Ingrid and I hadn't had a chance to talk properly after all the madness of the rehearsal and so we arranged to meet early the next morning before breakfast.

The sky was just glowing a warm, marmaladeyorange around the edges when we met beneath one of the towering oak trees. I pulled my gloves out of my coat pocket and shivered as the misty morning air coiled around me, like Otis the snake around his prey.

"Do we have to do this now?" grumbled Kip, stamping his feet and clutching his stomach. "It's freezing and I'm staaaaaarving."

"Yes, we do have to do it now," I said briskly. "We've got important matters of mystery to discuss. Derek Dweebles" – I paused dramatically – "is innocent!"

"Innocent?!" Kip goggled. "Are you sure?"

"Unfortunately, yes," I nodded. "He has an alibi for the fire; there's no way he could have started it."

Kip groaned. "But he was our top suspect."

We all went quiet then. "But if it isn't Derek Dweebles," Ingrid began, "then who is trying to sabotage the play? I mean, didn't you think it was suspicious that Gary was suddenly so sick?"

"You think someone poisoned him?!" I asked, wide-eyed.

"It wouldn't be too hard to slip something to make him sick into that cheese sandwich he was scoffing," said Ingrid.

"Well, that definitely rules out Dweebles," I pointed out. "He wasn't even in the hall until *after* Gary was ill."

We all stopped to think.

"This is the moment when Dougie Valentine would say, 'The plot thickens!' but I'm starting to think maybe that just means he doesn't know what is going on yet," I said glumly.

""What if. . ." Kip began tentatively.

"What?" I asked.

"Well, what if it is . . . you know . . . the Scottish Play thing. The witches. . ."

Ingrid snorted.

"No, something tells me there's a human hand at work here," I said finally. "And after all, if there's a dangerous criminal in our midst then finding them needs to be our priority."

They both nodded in agreement.

The bell rang, telling us it was time for breakfast, and the three of us headed in, deep in conversation about our case (or at least Ingrid and I did – Kip legged it towards his food like he was an Olympic athlete setting a new personal record).

Once we had sat down we were distracted from our happy chatter by Annabelle and her friends strolling past our table. I was hoping that this would be one of the times when we just ignored each other, but unfortunately Annabelle had other plans.

"There's Poppy Pym. I hear her weird non-family is coming to visit for Parents' Weekend," Annabelle said loudly to the girl next to her. "She's just so desperate for attention. It's sad really. I was telling Lucas all about her and we both laughed so much. He said it was totally pathetic."

"Oooooh!" gasped the gaggle of Lucas Quest fans who were following her around, their purple QFF badges glittering under the dining hall lights.

"What else did Lucas say?" breathed Trixie Pepperington-Wallop, one of Annabelle's most annoying sidekicks.

"Oh, just that she was a big show-off for someone who's such a loser." Annabelle's eyes flicked towards mine and a cruel smile tugged at her lips. "And that Parents' Weekend should really be limited to *actual* parents, not random clowns and circus freaks."

My mind grappled for a witty insult, but before I could do anything other than sit there with my mouth hanging open like a goldfish, they all bustled off with Annabelle talking loudly about how much Lucas liked her hair.

"Just ignore her," said Ingrid quietly as tears prickled at the back of my eyes. "She's just jealous. Everyone else is really excited that the circus is coming to Saint Smithen's."

"Yeah," chimed in Kip. "Don't pay any attention to Anna-smell. Everyone knows she's the worst."

"Thanks, guys," I snuffled. I felt shaky with anger and I had to admit that Annabelle had found a weak spot. Unfortunately, one look at her smug face told me that she knew it and that there was more to come. I wished that mention of Parents' Weekend didn't open a whole can of wormy feelings, wriggling away inside me.

"Anyway," said Ingrid brightly, "I thought we had a potential mystery to investigate!"

"You're right," I said, straightening my shoulders and standing up. "After all, Dougie Valentine wouldn't let a bully like Annabelle stand between him and a tricky case!" I pulled out my timetable and perked up at the sight of our first lesson. "Double music with Madame Patrice!" I exclaimed.

Kip's head hit the table with a thud.

"I thought you liked music lessons?" I asked.

"I do," Kip replied grudgingly, "but it means I have to lug that beast around." He pointed to the side of the room where a black case roughly the same size as Kip was leaning against the wall. It contained the tuba that Madame Patrice had decided Kip should learn to play. Kip actually wasn't a bad tuba player – after all, his big voice meant he was good at puffing out a nice, loud tune – but some of the *other* students thought he looked pretty funny playing an instrument that was almost the same size as his body. (Not me though, I would never think such a thing.) After the bell rang, we ran up the staircase to the music room (well, Ingrid and I began to run, but we had to slow down for a huffing Kip, thudding up each stair with his tuba case). Already the faint strains of squawking brass instruments and squealing violins were drifting down the corridor, and we pushed the door open to a scene of musical chaos. The classroom was full of instruments and students were encouraged to "have a go" at whatever they liked – which sometimes meant the music room didn't sound so musical.

In the middle of the room Madame Patrice lounged across a chaise longue. She wore a tight-fitting full-length silver evening gown that looked a bit like it had been made out of tin foil, and a long black cigarette holder hung empty in one languorous hand. She raised this to her crimson lips and inhaled, before crooning, "Daaaaaarlings!"

The room fell silent as Madame Patrice heaved herself to her feet. "Today we must get to work," she exclaimed. "As I shall reprise my celebrated role as Maria from *The Sound of Music*." Her eyes clouded over dreamily, and she was clearly reliving those glory days in her mind, a wide smile on her lipsticky lips.

"WE NEED NUNS!" she shouted suddenly, swivelling around in our direction. Kip dropped his tuba in fright.

Moments later Kip, Ingrid and I found ourselves wrapped in black scarves, swaying in the background and making "ah-ah-ah-ahhhh" noises while Madame Patrice spun around the room giving a rousing performance of "The Hills are Alive with the Sound of Music" and the rest of the class formed a ramshackle and slightly squeaky orchestra, ready for a run through of the whole production.

We had just got to the bit where Madame Patrice was weeping noisily over an uncomfortable-looking Kip who, as Mother Superior, was about to be forced to sing "Climb Every Mountain", when we were literally saved by the bell.

"PHEW!" exclaimed Kip, and I think we can safely say he spoke for all of us on that one. (Kip's singing voice is . . . "unique".)

Unfortunately our next lesson was chemistry with Miss Susan. Now I knew how Marie Antoinette felt as I dragged my feet all the way to the science lab, feeling like a noble queen off to meet her executioner. When we got there, however, Miss Susan was nowhere to be seen. We all took our usual seats and a quiet hum of chatter filled the air.

Suddenly I heard one dreaded voice pipe up loudly above the crowd. "Of course, Mummy and Daddy are so excited about meeting Lucas. They are all going to get along like a house on fire." Annabelle giggled. "Oops! Poor choice of words!" Her posse of friends all laughed dutifully. "It's such a nice tradition, Parents' Weekend," Annabelle continued airily, but I could feel a fiery ball of anxiety growing in my chest. "So nice to have your parents come and visit." Her eyes met mine and they sparkled gleefully. Everyone else had gone quiet by now, and Annabelle's lilting voice filled the room. "Oh sorry, Poppy!" she exclaimed, her eyes widening dramatically. "I forgot that you don't actually have any parents. This must be a hard time for you."

I cleared my throat, trying not to sound like I was about to cry. "Actually, my whole family will be coming," I managed, and there were a few murmurs of excitement around the classroom.

Annabelle held my gaze like a snake about to strike at its prey. "But they're not your real family, are they?" she asked softly. "Your real parents didn't even want you. They just dumped you with a bunch of strangers, like a piece of rubbish."

CHAPTER TWENTY-ONE

It felt exactly like falling from the trapeze in my nightmare. WHOOSH! Only this time I didn't wake up. All the air was knocked out of me, and all the feelings that I had been so carefully pushing down rushed up to the surface and crashed over me. A hard cold voice rang in my head. *Your parents didn't want you.* Hot tears rushed to my eyes and I could only watch as if in slow motion as Kip and Ingrid sprang to their feet.

"Annabelle!" A voice cut through the room like a knife. I turned to see Miss Susan standing in the doorway, and for a second she seemed to be alight, to blaze with big, fiery anger. Then, almost immediately, the shutters came down and that fire was gone. She said in her cool voice, "That is enough. Your behaviour is unacceptable. Please report to Miss Baxter's office immediately."

Annabelle stood up, her cheeks slightly flushed, and flounced to the door. The cold, hard smile that she gave me on her way past told me that she knew her attack had hit me hard. I could only gulp back the tears as Miss Susan carried on with the lesson as if nothing had happened. Ingrid reached over and squeezed my hand and Kip, looking furious, had slipped his book of practical jokes into his chemistry textbook and was turning the pages, muttering darkly.

By the time the lesson had finished my stomach was still churning away like I was looping-the-loop on my own personal rollercoaster. I tried as hard as I could to squish my worries about Parents' Weekend and family and the whole whirlwind of thoughts and feelings back into the box that my brain usually kept them in, but Annabelle's words kept coming back to me. I couldn't help but think maybe she was right. My parents must not have wanted me or why would they have left me at the circus? What was so wrong with me?

Kip and Ingrid were extra nice to me for the rest

of the day, and Kip even offered me his jam sponge after lunch – although the relief on his face when I said no would have been obvious from space. Having them around helped me to feel better and I did my best to act as though what Annabelle had said hadn't really bothered me, although I couldn't quite silence that nasty voice in my head.

At least I had the distraction of a visit to Penny's house after school to keep me occupied. As promised, she had managed to sweet-talk Miss Baxter into letting us go and visit her for tea on the proviso that Mr Grant took us down to Brimwell and picked us up in the minibus. I know we were all hoping that this chat with Penny would reveal some further clues about Phineas Scrimshaw and his lost gold. Plus it was exciting to have a free pass to leave school grounds after lessons had finished.

At four thirty on the dot Mr Grant dropped us off outside Penny's Parlour. "Right, you lot," he said with the easy smile that scrunched up the scar on the side of his face, "I'll be back for you in two hours . . . got it?"

We all nodded eagerly.

"And Miss Farthing has asked me to pick you up from the bus stop at the end of the road. OK?"

We nodded again. *What could Penny have in store*, I wondered. It looked like we would soon find out because the woman herself had emerged from the shop to greet us. We jumped out and waved to Mr Grant as the minibus tootled back up the high street towards the school.

"Welcome!" cried Penny, clutching each of us to her chest in turn. "Come in, come in!" She bustled us into the shop.

We had never been in Penny's Parlour before and the effect was instant and overwhelming.

"Agh!" shrieked Kip.

"Everything all right, dear?" Penny asked, looking concerned.

"Yes, sorry," Kip replied shakily. "It's just ... a lot ... of cats."

Kip was not wrong. There were cats everywhere. A couple of them were real and snoozing or slinking about the shop, but most of them stared out from plates, mugs, T-shirts, jumpers, curtains, cushions, jewellery, paintings, photographs, pencil cases, and really, pretty much anything else you can think of. If you could put a cat's face on it then Penny sold it.

"Oh yes!" Penny sounded delighted. "It's the

largest collection of cat-based collectibles for miles around! Takes your breath away really, doesn't it?"

"Y-yes," choked out Ingrid. "It truly does."

"Now, let's go upstairs for a spot of tea." Penny shut the door to the shop firmly behind us and turned the cat-shaped sign from "OPEN" to "CLOSED". "I'm closing a little bit early today for my guests of honour!" With that she led us through the back of the shop and up a flight of creaky stairs.

We followed her into a little flat, stuffed with more cat-related objects and a familiar black cat, lying on an elaborate bed in front of a merry fire. "There he is!" Penny cried, plucking up the poor cat from his perfectly comfortable position and stuffing him into my arms. "Little Buttons! He's so eager to thank you!"

The cat was squalling in my ear and wriggling in a way that contradicted Penny's statement but I tried my best to look pleased. "Now, I'll go and get the tea!" she tinkled as she bustled out of the room.

With a sigh of relief I let go of the wriggling cat and he stalked back over to his bed, giving me a very *un*grateful look.

Kip was staring around with a horrified expression on his face. "What IS this place?" he gasped. "It's like something from a horror movie!"

I had to admit that the effect of the light from the fire flickering on all the cats' faces around the room was quite alarming. Buttons let out a long MEOOOOOW as if he was in total agreement.

Penny reappeared, carrying a fully loaded tea tray and this certainly seemed to take the edge off Kip's unhappiness. "Sit down! Sit down!" she sang, and we all unbuttoned our coats and sat on the squashy sofa. From down here the cat faces weren't so overwhelming and I sneakily stuffed a couple of cat cushions behind my back, reducing the number I could see even further. Penny sat down in an armchair across from us and poured out four steaming cups of tea before passing around a plate of freshly toasted hot buttered crumpets.

"Maybe it's not so bad," Kip whispered to me, munching his way through his third crumpet in under two minutes.

"Penny," I said, as she was refilling my teacup for the second time. "Did you say that you had some papers and things that might help with our project on Phineas Scrimshaw?" I darted a look at Kip and Ingrid and they both sat forward a little.

Penny smiled. "Yes I did, and I put them all in a box for you," she said. "Here it is," and she pulled a small shoebox out from under her armchair and opened it up. We delved inside pulling things out. There was a family tree, a few newspaper clippings and some photographs but they were all about Scrimshaws that lived much later than Phineas. Finally, from the bottom of the box, Ingrid pulled out a thin and delicate-looking pamphlet.

"What's this?" she asked Penny.

"Oh, that's just a list of the items in his collection. In fact, that is another real tragedy about the town hall fire," Penny said with a sigh. "All of his collection burnt to a crisp. They say that's where the fire started, you know – in the exhibition where all of his most prized items were on display."

"That's so sad," I said. "What was in his collection?"

"Oh, such interesting things from his travels." Penny sighed again. "All sorts of fossils and specimens – he was a very big collector. Fascinated by natural science. It was a wonderful resource for the community. Well, you can see the list there." Ingrid peered closely at the list and then slipped it back into the box for safekeeping.

"Not a lot on Phineas Scrimshaw, then," I said, trying to keep the disappointment out of my voice.

"I know," said Penny, patting my knee. "When I went through the papers again I realized they might not be much help for your project. So I thought perhaps you would like a little outing?"

"An outing?" I asked, puzzled. "Where?"

"I'm afraid Mr Grant will be here to pick us up soon," said Ingrid.

"Well, luckily we're just going up the road!" said Penny, brightly. "I thought you might like to go and see the man himself!"

"You mean. . ." I began.

"Yes," said Penny, "the final resting place of Phineas Scrimshaw – Saint Smithen's cemetery."

CHAPTER TWENTY-TWO

It had already been quite a strange visit so a trip to the cemetery didn't seem that odd, all things considered. It turned out that Penny had bought a nice bunch of flowers and she thought we might like to go and put them on Scrimshaw's grave. I actually thought the idea was quite sweet. Kip didn't look so sure. Especially when Penny revealed her final surprise.

Before we left the flat she handed each of us a parcel, wrapped in cat-covered wrapping paper. Inside each one was a soft, snuggly purple jumper with a cat's face knitted on it. "Just another little gift to say thank you!" she whispered to me as I gave her a quick hug. Ingrid and I pulled the jumpers on. I actually thought they were kind of cool. Then I turned to face Kip. He was looking at the jumper like Penny had given him a bag of cat sick. "Kip!" I whispered out of the side of my mouth. "Don't be rude!"

Kip plastered on a smile. "Thanks, Penny!" he said in a loud voice. "That's really . . . great."

"Well, aren't you going to put it on?" Penny asked. "It's cold outside, you know!"

The smile remained frozen on Kip's face as I could see him mentally running through all of his options. After a couple of seconds he obviously realized he couldn't get out of it without looking really rude so he tugged the fluffy jumper over his head. Unfortunately, to add insult to injury, the purple sleeves fell way down over his hands and he was forced to push them up around his elbows.

"A little big," said Penny critically, "but you'll grow into it I'm sure. I'm afraid it's the smallest size we sell."

"Thank you," ground out Kip, the smile still on his face but murder in his eyes.

"Well," I said brightly, "let's go, shall we!"

We pottered down the high street and I was pleased to see that Brimwell had added twinkling orange lights to its already brilliant Halloween display, and they hung overhead, wrapped around lamp posts and strewn across shopfronts. I snuggled into my fluffy jumper, and even Kip seemed glad to be wearing his as the cold evening air bit at us like a hungry vampire.

Saint Smithen's church was set back slightly from the road, its single spire looming up into the night sky. As we made our way down the path into the cemetery I heard Kip mutter to Ingrid, "This is seriously spooky!"

Kip was right again. It was six o'clock and nearly dark. There were a couple of street lamps shining in the cemetery, but these just seemed to create a load of creepy, hulking shadows. I jumped at the sound of something rustling in a nearby tree, and strained my eyes against the murky twilight. Everything was very quiet as Penny came to a stop in front of a very simple headstone.

HERE LIES
PHINEAS SCRIMSHAW
A GOOD AND HONEST MAN.

We stood for a moment in silence. It was strange

to think that the real Phineas Scrimshaw was buried right here, underneath us. Strange *and* a bit frightening.

"It's not a very fancy grave," I whispered as Penny bent down to leave her flowers.

"No," Penny agreed. "Not quite what you would expect for a lord, is it? Still, after his death there wasn't a lot of money to pay for his funeral. The people in the town paid for this headstone. He was actually very well liked ... outside of his own family, of course."

"Don't you ever wonder about it," I asked her, "being his last remaining descendant and all?"

"The gold, you mean?" Penny asked. I nodded. Penny shook her head. "Now what would I want with that when I've already got everything a woman could ask for?" We smiled at each other. "Oh, look at the time!" Penny exclaimed. "We'd better get down to the bus stop; Mr Grant will be waiting!"

We made our way back on to the high street and towards the bus stop. Across the road the shadowy skeleton of the town hall looked almost normal in the low light. "So sad," Penny muttered, shaking her head.

"We'll just have to hope that the play raises

loads of money," said Ingrid comfortingly. Kip and I nodded in agreement, looking up at the big old building that had survived so much.

We were at the bus stop now, but there was no sign of Mr Grant yet. Suddenly, something caught my eye. "What's that?" I said, pointing to a nearby shrub. Something seemed to be twinkling in the light of the street lamps.

"IS IT A GHOST?" yelled Kip, who still didn't seem very comfortable with the idea of roaming around cemeteries at night.

"No," I said, reaching in gently and feeling around. I gave the object a tug and pulled out a purple leopard-print cat carrier.

"Buttons's carry case!" Penny exclaimed. "But how on earth did that get there?! It's the one I lost in the fire!"

"Are you sure it's the same one?" I asked and Penny turned to me as if I was mad.

"Well, *of course* it's the same one!" she said firmly. "Magda made it for me. It's *bespoke*. It has BUTTONS written around the front in pink rhinestones." She swivelled the case around so that we could see the sparkling stones which had been the source of the twinkling.

"Lovely," Ingrid murmured. Kip opened his mouth to say something but luckily he caught my eye first and chose to keep his comments to himself instead.

"But how on earth did it end up in this bush?" Penny looked confused, and I knew just how she felt. It seemed to me that this must be an important clue, but I couldn't for the life of me work out how it was supposed to fit in.

Penny opened the little door on the front. "Eugh!" she cried. "What is this?" She handed me the case and I peered inside. The material was singed in places and covered in blobs of white wax.

"Has someone been melting candles in here?" I asked.

"Candles? This is just getting stranger and stranger." Penny shook her head. "Well, anyway," she said, "it's totally ruined. What a shame."

"Do you mind if I keep hold of it?" I asked. Whatever this case was doing here I was sure it was a valuable piece of evidence in our investigation.

Penny looked surprised. "No, I don't mind. But what do you want it for?"

"Oh, er, just an art project," I said quickly.

"Oh, right," Penny said, but our conversation was interrupted by the swoop of shining headlamps and

179

Mr Grant appeared in the minibus.

"Thanks so much for having us!" I wheezed as I was pulled into another bone-crushing embrace.

"And the jumpers!" said Ingrid before being squished into her own suffocating cuddle.

"Thanks for the crumpets!" said Kip, darting into the bus faster than a speeding bullet in order to avoid any more hugging.

Penny waved as we drove off, and I stared at the cat carrier in my arms. It had disappeared during the fire so I knew it was important, but why? What *was* all this wax from? And *how* did the carrier end up by the bus stop? It was a real puzzler.

When we arrived back at the school Miss Baxter was waiting out front for us.

"Sorry, children, but I need to borrow Poppy for a while," she said, her hand on my shoulder already guiding me towards her office.

"Am I in trouble?" I asked, holding the cat carrier out for Ingrid, so she could take it back to our room.

"Not this time." Miss Baxter grinned.

Kip and Ingrid looked questioningly in my direction, but I could only shrug silently and follow after her.

CHAPTER TWENTY-THREE

Outside Miss Baxter's office the same blonde woman was sitting at the assistant's desk, painting her fingernails the colour of pink custard. She snapped her gum a couple of times as we approached, but otherwise didn't really acknowledge our existence.

"Cynthia," Miss Baxter piped up after an awkward moment. "This is one of our first year students – Poppy Pym."

I waved one hand, and Cynthia's eyes flicked in my direction. "Yeah," she muttered, her concentration returning to her fingernails. "Nice to meet you, Polly."

"It's PoPPy—" I began, but Miss Baxter shook her head.

"Any messages?" Miss Baxter asked patiently.

"Oh, yeah." Cynthia nodded. "A bunch of people called about some stuff. I can't really remember to be honest. They weren't, like, the most interesting bunch, you know?" She gingerly picked up a pink post-it note covered in scrawl. "Here's some of them." She handed them to me. "WATCH THE NAILS!" she hissed.

"Er, thanks," I said, looking at the post-it uncertainly.

"I'll take that, thank you!" Miss Baxter plucked it from my hands. "Now, come on, Poppy, there's something I need to show you," and she pushed me towards her office door.

All thoughts of assistants vanished once I stepped into Miss Baxter's office because standing inside was my whole family. With a squeak I threw myself into Pym's open arms and buried my head in her shoulder. She smelled of rose soap and spun sugar and I felt tears stinging at the back of my eyes as she wrapped me in a warm, familiar hug.

"I told you it would be good surprise, eh, Tomato?" Fanella's voice reached my ears.

"I thought you weren't arriving until tomorrow?" I gasped as I was pulled into a body-squishing hug with Boris, then squeezed between Doris and Marvin.

"We couldn't wait!" squeaked BoBo, as Chuckles fell at my feet and offered me a rose he had made out of balloons.

"Where's Buttercup?" I asked, looking around.

"Miss Baxter thought it might not be a good idea to have her wandering around in case she caught someone unawares, so she's curled up in her bed in Luigi's trailer," said Sharp-Eye Sheila, her arm around Luigi's shoulder. I noticed that Luigi had a large plaster stuck across his top lip, covering the right-hand side of his moustache.

"Anyway," said Tina, "we wanted to make sure—"

"—We got here in plenty of time before the rehearsal," finished Tawna.

"We missed you!" they exclaimed in unison, squeezing me in between them like a Poppy sandwich.

"It's so good of you all to step in," said Miss Baxter, clasping her hands together. "It would have been such a shame to cancel when we could raise so much money for the town hall, and there's a lot of local press interest as well, because of the fire."

"Yes, Miss Baxter has been telling us all about it," said Pym, fixing me with her all-seeing stare. "It sounds like we have lots to catch up on."

I squirmed a bit at that but luckily Fanella's loud voice cut in.

"Me, I will play main character, yes?" she demanded.

There was a brief silence.

"Um, no," I said eventually, "they already have someone to play Macbeth. And he's . . . a man."

"No problem." Fanella clicked her fingers. "I wear the false moostache."

Luigi flinched and touched the plaster on his top lip. A sound like a muffled sob escaped him.

"No, no," I said hurriedly, "but you can play one of the three witches if you like?"

Fanella glared at me. "You want me to play a weetch? What are you saying, Tomato? You think I am like weetch?"

Fortunately we were interrupted by a knock at the door.

"Come in!" called Miss Baxter in a relieved voice.

The door opened to reveal Inspector Hartley. I hadn't seen the inspector since our little run-in with an international jewel thief, but he still seemed to be wearing the same crumpled suit, and his grey eyes were fixed on Miss Baxter's face.

"Arthur!" Miss Baxter exclaimed, a pink glow

spilling across her freckled cheeks.

"Sorry I'm late, Emma—" he began, but stopped when he saw the entire circus troupe staring at him.

"No, no," Miss Baxter waved a hand, "I'm quite behind and I was distracted by the arrival of Poppy's family." She paused. "You remember Poppy? And the rest of Madame Pym's travelling circus?"

"How could I forget? How do you do, Miss Pym?" He turned to me. "I hear you're caught up in my investigation again? Volunteering with the drama society, are you?" I nodded and his piercing gaze made me feel like Pym wasn't the only one who could read people's minds. "I understand that you are all stepping in to help out?" he continued, turning to Pym.

"Yes we are," Pym said slowly, "and I think you may shortly be getting some of the answers you are looking for, Inspector." Her eyes had taken on that cloudy look that meant she was seeing something that the rest of us couldn't.

"Well," the Inspector said briskly, "I was going to ask if you would mind me popping in to your rehearsal tomorrow?"

"Not at all," Pym muttered. "In fact, I think that would be a very good idea."

CHAPTER TWENTY-FOUR

The next day it was a much smaller group of players that met in the great hall for rehearsal. I led my family in and the room fell quiet. (I had to admit that my noisy, colourful circus troupe did seem to stick out a bit in the grand old hall – not that it seemed to bother them much.) Letty barrelled over, her trusty walkie-talkie clipped to her side. "Hello, everyone," she greeted my family. "I'm Letty; I don't know if you remember me?" She didn't wait for a reply. "But I'll be in charge of scenery, lighting, all your stage management requirements. I can assure you, my team are ready." She pointed towards a group of students dressed all in black, just like Letty, standing in a neat line and staring straight ahead like soldiers. "It took me a while," said Letty seriously, "but now I have them working like a well-oiled machine."

"Thank you very much, Letty," said Pym, "that is very reassuring."

Letty gave her team a small nod and, as one, they all saluted, turned around and marched off, their walkie-talkies gleaming at their sides.

"OK." Pym clapped her hands and everyone gathered around. "It's nice to see you all here. I know that there have been some complications, but I am confident that we can get things smoothed out by Sunday."

She was interrupted by the arrival of Maxwell Dangerfield who grabbed Pym's shoulders and kissed her loudly on both cheeks. "Madame Director!" he cried. "A thousand apologies for my lateness. It is so good of you to step in. I am so thrilled that you will be the one to guide us safely from these troubled seas into calmer shores—"

Pym fixed Maxwell with her knowing stare and he faltered slightly. "Ah – " he spoke more quietly now, "I think you will find us in reasonable shape, although we are short a couple of witches."

"Well, as to that," Pym spoke with authority, "Sharp-Eye Sheila and Doris here have agreed to step in. They already know all the lines." I noticed Fanella standing with her arms folded and a furious look on her face, and I moved slightly further away from her. "And everyone else – " Pym gestured "is here to help however they can. So let's get started with a run-through, shall we?"

The rehearsal began and I had to say that Maxwell Dangerfield was good – perhaps it was a shame he was no longer acting. Lucas was really going for it in the role of Banquo – they were almost trying to out-act each other. I was so engrossed in the performances that it took me a while to realize I was standing next to a lady I hadn't met before. She had tanned skin and her dark hair was peppered with grey.

"Wonderful, isn't he?" she whispered to me, her eyes on Maxwell Dangerfield. I murmured in agreement. "I used to adore him in *All Tomorrow's Yesterdays*," she continued. "I watched it every afternoon. It's fabulous to see him acting again – he hasn't really been in anything after they killed him off that show. I loved it when he played his own evil twin sister. Of course," she giggled, leaning towards me, "I knew him before he was famous. Used to go to school with him, right here!"

"I didn't know Maxwell went to Saint Smithen's!" I exclaimed.

"Oh, yes. But then, he wasn't called Maxwell Dangerfield then – he changed that when he became an actor. His real name is Arthur Scroggins."

"Arthur Scroggins?" I spluttered. "No wonder he changed it! I'm Poppy Pym, by the way," I whispered.

"Lucia Quest." She smiled. "I'm Lucas's mum."

"Oh!" I was surprised. She seemed much nicer than Lucas Quest. "You must be very proud of him," I murmured.

"Oh yes!" she said proudly. "It's wonderful that he's done so well. Although it's a lot of work – and not just for him." She shrugged. "Lots of early starts and travelling for me too. And helping him with his lines and looking after all his costumes and things, it's a full-time job. Why, the other day he came in *covered* in fake blood from some big scene he was in and it was a nightmare to get all of that red paint out of his clothes and off of his hands." She shook her head. "He doesn't like me coming to watch really, but I snuck in today. It's so nice to meet some of

189

his friends." She smiled at me again but I could feel the wheels inside my head cranking around and a buzzing filled my ears.

"Covered in blood?" I asked slowly. "What day was that?"

Lucia frowned. "Um, let me see . . . it would have been . . . Monday, I think. Why?"

At that moment though I was distracted by an astonishing sight – that of Pym hurling herself like a human cannonball on to the stage and pushing Maxwell to the ground.

"Ooof!" he groaned. "Why did you do—" but his protests were cut short by an ominous creaking noise. With an almighty groan one of the chandeliers the art department had made for the set broke from the rope that was holding it and crashed on to the stage, smashing right on to the spot where Maxwell had been standing.

We all stared at the shattered pieces for a moment in stunned silence. Maxwell Dangerfield's face had gone the colour of a glass of skimmed milk, and the whole room stood frozen as if someone had put us on pause.

Then the pretty, dark-haired woman playing Lady Macbeth burst into noisy tears and fled down the steps from the stage and straight out of the door, screeching something about us all being doomed – and everyone seemed to come back to life. People crowded around Maxwell, helping him to his feet and asking if he was OK. Lucas's mum ran up on to the stage and towards her son. He was standing stock still and gazing at the shards of chandelier, his face pale and his mouth in a tight line.

I hurried up on to the stage as well. "Letty," I asked her quietly. "Can someone lower the rope? The rope that held the chandelier?"

With a trembling hand, Letty reached for her walkie-talkie and muttered into it. The rope began to drop to where I stood beneath it.

"As I suspected," I whispered to myself, holding the rope in my hand and looking closely at the neat ends. "This rope has been cut."

My eyes travelled over the group of people huddled around Maxwell and Pym, all talking loudly over the top of one another. The hamster wheel of my brain was spinning so furiously I felt a bit dizzy. The rope that I was holding in my hand only confirmed my suspicions. This was a deliberate act of sabotage. And I knew who was behind it.

CHAPTER TWENTY-FIVE

It was all so clear to me now. I had solved the case. I basked in the glory of being a true detective for a moment before shaking myself out of a daydream in which Inspector Hartley was calling me a hero and offering me a shining medal, and realized that a heated argument was taking place between Maxwell and Pym.

"How can we *possibly* continue?" Maxwell cried. "Another near-fatal accident! Another leading character has just pulled out! This play is truly cursed. How can we possibly be ready in two days, and with all the local press coming..." He drifted off, a haunted look in his eyes.

"The play *will* go on," said Pym firmly. "And it will be a great success." When Pym uses that tone of voice it is impossible to argue with her – she just sounds so utterly certain.

"OK, OK, you have twisted my arms." Fanella rose to her feet. "I shall do it."

There was a pause. "Do what, dear?" asked Doris.

"I will play the lady star character," Fanella answered majestically.

Luigi let out a great guffaw, but when Fanella turned her furious face towards him he tried to turn it into a coughing fit.

"But my dear," said Maxwell anxiously, "do you know the part? This is one of the most difficult and complex roles in the whole of Shakespeare."

"Of course," Fanella answered immediately with a dismissive wave of her hand. "Is easy. This Shakespeare, he is quite OK, I think. He does lots of killings in his plays. Is hilarious."

Maxwell looked more worried than ever at this answer.

Fanella stomped on to the stage and stood across from him. "Unfirm porpoises!" she shouted, clasping her hands in front of her. "Give me all your knives." She grabbed at the air. "Sleeping people and dead people are in the pictures," she cried, sinking to the ground.

I was flicking through the script trying to work out where Fanella was, when Doris whispered in my ear. "She means, 'Infirm of purpose! Give me the daggers. The sleeping and the dead are but as pictures.' Act Two, Scene Two."

I looked at Doris in surprise, but she just picked up her knitting and clacked the needles.

"It is those creepy children with the eyeholes who are afraid of paintings and also devils," Fanella screeched, throwing herself on the ground.

"'Tis the eye of childhood that fears a painted devil," whispered Doris between stitches.

There was a long moment of uncertain silence and then Maxwell started clapping slowly. "Brava!" he cried. "Spectacular! Such *passion*!"

"Bah," said Fanella, but a pleased smile tugged at the corners of her mouth.

"My dear, you are a triumph!" he said, staring moonily at her face.

Fanella shrugged. "I know. This what I keep telling you," she sighed.

"With us in the leads the play will be an enormous success!" Maxwell shook his fist and everyone cheered.

The rehearsal continued for another hour and it

really did seem as though things were going better. I know people always think *Macbeth* is a big tragedy but I don't think they can really be understanding all those funny words Shakespeare uses because, let me tell you, Fanella was right. It was hilarious. And when Inspector Hartley slipped into a seat at the back of the room, he appeared to think so as well. At least, his shoulders kept shaking and he seemed to be trying pretty hard not to laugh the whole time, probably so as not to distract the actors.

Anyway, Kip, Ingrid and I were kept busy for the rest of the rehearsal, making sure that the props were all in order and that everything was on stage at the right time. For the first time, just like Letty's crew, we were running like a well-oiled machine. And all that time I was itching to tell them what I had deduced.

When Pym finally called the run-through to an end, everyone seemed relieved to have got through the whole play without any more incidents. We were certainly all a bit jumpy and Kip's enthusiastic drum banging had caused a minor kafuffle when Miss Marigold had dropped her prop sword in fright.

"Inspector," Pym said with a smile, spotting

Inspector Hartley, "perhaps you would like to join us for dinner?"

The inspector looked pleased and then his face fell. "I would love to, Madame Pym," he said, "but I'm afraid I must get back to the station – reports to file, you know." He sounded tired and a bit fed up, and who could blame him? I decided that when I was a grown-up detective I wouldn't bother with any boring reports – it would just be all action, all the time.

"And Poppy," said Pym, "Miss Baxter said you and your friends can have dinner with us if you like?"

"YES!" crowed Kip, visions of candyfloss clearly dancing before his eyes.

"Sounds brilliant," I agreed.

"Thank you," beamed Ingrid, her big eyes shining.

As we wandered down to the circus camp Pym pulled my arm through hers. "And then maybe you can fill us in on this big mystery!" she said.

Once we were back at the circus camp we found that Marvin had set up an excellent campfire, and Boris was busy barbequing dozens of sausages and burgers, which smelled amazing. We all huddled around the fire, snuggled up in our coats and ate sausages and beans off paper plates as the first stars began to peek out. When Boris pulled out a bag of marshmallows almost the size of me, Kip groaned with happiness.

"This is how to live," he murmured, leaning back and rubbing his full belly.

Kip was right, and it was easy to forget, sitting here laughing and joking with my family, that we had a case to solve. But I had a theory, and I needed to talk to them all about it. I cleared my throat and then began by filling everyone in on all the details of the fire at the town hall, our suspicions about Derek Dweebles and his alibi.

"But if the Dweebles did not do it, Tomato, then who is the criminal?" Fanella asked.

"Someone else who had something to gain," I said.

"Was it this cat lady?" asked Luigi, rubbing Buttercup's tummy. "She sounds a bit dotty in the brain box to me. Fancy being so obsessed with a cat." He snorted.

"No, I don't think it was Penny," I said.

"Was it a ghost?" asked Boris, looking a bit scared.

"Oh, no, Poppy," squeaked BoBo, "I hate ghosts."

"You no need be afraid," said Fanella. "For keep away ghosts you must only have garlics."

"That's for—" Tawna began.

"—Werewolves," finished Tina.

"Of course it's not for ghosts or werewolves," cried an exasperated Marvin. "Everyone knows garlic is for keeping away vampires."

"No," said Fanella. "Is ghosts. They say 'Yuk, we no like these garlics' and then they fly away. Is old Italian folktale," she finished.

Everyone groaned. "Well, now we know it's not for ghosts," said Sharp-Eye Sheila. "You only ever say it's an 'old Italian folktale' when you've made something up."

"How DARE YOU insult my ancestors! I curse you with the old Italian ways!" Fanella leapt to her feet, her eyes blazing, and she began speaking in very fast, very angry, Italian and waving her hands around in a lot of not-very-polite gestures.

"It wasn't a ghost!" I yelled. "Or a werewolf, or a vampire."

"Well, then who was it?" Sharp-Eye Sheila asked.

I took a deep breath. "Well, actually, I suppose it was a vampire, of sorts."

"A vampire!" screamed Kip, jumping to his feet.

"I KNEW IT! I KNEW THERE WAS SOMETHING
SPOOKY GOING ON!"

"No," I said impatiently, "not a real vampire. A
love vampire," I looked around at the puzzled faces,
as all except Ingrid looked completely confused. "As
in *Love Vampire: A Vampire in Love*." Still nothing.
Finally I gave up. "The fire," I said slowly, "was
started by Lucas Quest."

CHAPTER TWENTY-SIX

Three marshmallows fell out of Kip's mouth.

"Lucas Quest?" he mumbled through the two remaining marshmallows.

"Yes." I nodded confidently.

"I never like that boy," said Fanella. "I knew he was ghost."

"He isn't a ghost," I said, pressing my hand to my forehead. "He's just a boy."

"Why do you think Lucas did it, Poppy?" Pym asked gently.

"OK," I said, standing up. "First of all, I spoke to his mum today. She said that he came home from rehearsal covered in blood."

"Blood?" Boris looked a bit queasy.

"Not real blood," I said, impatiently.

"What day was this?" asked Ingrid beadily.

"Monday," I said, and I saw the light dawning in her eyes.

"What's that got to do with anything?" asked Kip, reaching for another handful of marshmallows. "There's loads of fake blood in the performance. Letty made sure of that."

"But not on Monday," I said quickly. "Monday was the first day of rehearsals – we didn't have any props yet or fake blood. It was, however, the day the warning appeared – written in wet red paint."

Ingrid jumped to her feet. "And Lucas refused to take off his coat and gloves," her eyes sparkled, "because they must have been covered in paint. Just like Lady Macbeth, he couldn't wash the red paint off. How pleasing," she said to herself.

"And he came in a bit late and was all touchy when Dweebles asked where he had been, remember?" I said.

Kip nodded and stuffed another marshmallow in his face, his eyes wide. "You're right!" he said. (Or at least I think he did. It sounded more like "Murr Miggh!")

"And Lucas could easily have poisoned Gary;

he was the one chatting with him before the performance. He could definitely have slipped something into his sandwich," I pointed out.

"But why would he do these things?" asked Fanella.

"And none of this explains why you think he started the fire," said Marvin.

"Penny said he wasn't with them when the fire started!" I exclaimed. "She said he went off with Maxwell, having an argument but he could easily have slipped away."

"But *why*?" asked Ingrid. "Why would Lucas sabotage the play?"

"Don't you see?" I cried. "He wasn't sabotaging the play; he was getting rid of the actors, working his way up into a starring role! He used the fire to get the publicity and make everyone think the play was cursed. Then to really terrify people he left that horrible message, so that Banquo left in panic and he got his part. He poisoned Gary's sandwich, hoping that his trick would work twice. When all the local reporters came to the play it would be to see him in the lead part; only he couldn't predict that Maxwell would decide to play Macbeth himself. So today he put another plan into motion. He knew exactly where Maxwell would be standing in that scene, right underneath the chandelier, so earlier he sneaked in and cut the rope that held it, apart from just a few strands. All he had to do was stall the scene until the rope snapped and the part would be his!"

I finished my speech and everyone sat in round-eyed silence.

"I can't believe it!" Ingrid exclaimed. "He could have killed Maxwell!"

"No," I shook my head, "it was only papier-mâché. It would have given him a nasty knock, but it wouldn't have killed him."

"I think it all makes sense," said Pym. "Too much sense to be a coincidence. But the trouble is you don't have any evidence."

I sank back into my seat. "I know," I admitted, "and I don't know how to get any."

"We make him confess," said Fanella, calmly examining her fingernails. "Boris have ways of making him talk." Boris cracked his knuckles ominously.

"*Obviously* we can't do that," I said, shaking my head. Kip looked disappointed.

"I get you, Tomato." Fanella gave me an elaborate wink. "OBVIOUSLY we CAN'T do that."

"That's right," I said. "We can't. Obviously."

"Yes. Riiiiight." Fanella winked again, and I shook my head.

"Actually, I think I might have an idea," I said slowly. I whispered a question in Marvin's ear.

Marvin looked thoughtful. "Will Lucas be here for Parents' Weekend?" he asked.

"Yes," I replied. "His fan club were chattering about it. He's going to meet Annabelle's parents."

Marvin nodded and rubbed his hands together gleefully.

"Well Luigi, I think you'd better start learning Banquo's lines," I said, sweeping my arms forward in a dramatic gesture.

"Eh?!" said Luigi, looking panicky. "No, no old gal, more of a background figure myself. Play a soldier or a tree if you like, but not a big part like that."

"I'll do it," boomed Boris. "Always fancied myself as an actor. Not keen on the name Banquo though... What about Boris?"

"Fine, fine," I grumbled, "you're ruining my dramatic moment. What I'm saying is that someone needs to be ready to step in for Lucas because I've got a plan to make him confess everything. And we'll do it tomorrow!"

CHAPTER TWENTY-SEVEN

The next morning was the start of Parents' Weekend and it dawned crisp and clear. My insides were trembling with excitement over the plans we had for the day.

All this excitement wasn't quite drowning out the sad feelings that I had about today, and that I still hadn't talked about with Pym. That felt pretty horrible. Usually I could talk to Pym about anything, but talking to her about my parents felt wrong somehow, as if talking about them meant that I didn't really love my family, or like I didn't think that they were enough for me. I couldn't bear the idea of upsetting Pym. I might not call her "Mum" but she was the best mother I could ask for. It was a pretty jumbly, sad, grey feeling, and I didn't know how to make things better.

In her own way, Ingrid also had mixed feelings about Parents' Weekend. "I love my parents," she groaned after we met Kip outside in the entrance hall, "but they're so embarrassing."

Kip had been uncharacteristically quiet about the whole thing.

"What about your parents, Kip?" I looked over at him. "What time do they get here?"

"Oh, they're not coming," he said lightly.

"Not coming?" I frowned, crinkling my forehead.

"Why not?" Ingrid asked, her face concerned.

"Just couldn't make it, I guess," Kip said, avoiding our eyes. "They're really busy, you know. They were really sorry about it. They'll be at the next one." His smile didn't quite reach his eyes.

"Well," I said cheerfully, "you can always just hang out with us. Plenty of room for one more at the circus. Plus," I added, with a sneaky look at Ingrid, "Boris said he reckoned you were on track to become a great strongman."

"Really?" Kip's head snapped up and he looked closely at my face. I plastered on my best angelic smile.

"Absolutely," chimed in Ingrid. "He said you were obviously getting stronger. And taller."

Kip's face lit up. "Well, I did show him my chart," he said very seriously. "And Boris said that being half a centimetre taller made all the difference."

"Exactly," I said, nodding in agreement.

"Precisely," Ingrid echoed, and we both smiled sweetly.

Kip looked at his watch. "I'm starving," he said. "Are we going in for breakfast, or what?"

Ingrid and I shared a look of relief and a secret, silent high five behind Kip's back before we all bustled into the dining hall.

Parents started arriving after breakfast and I was excited to meet Ingrid's mum and dad. Ingrid's mum looked like a grown-up version of Ingrid but without the glasses. She was very tall and thin with long, pale blonde hair and big, pale blue eyes that looked a bit dreamy. Ingrid's dad was much shorter, with thin mousy hair and – like Ingrid – thick spectacles that made his blue eyes look enormous.

"Hello, children," Ingrid's mum said. "Nice to see you again."

"Mum," said Ingrid with a sigh. "You've never

met them before. This is Kip and Poppy. My best friends."

"Nice to meet you," said Ingrid's dad shortly. He was peering around the entrance hall where we were standing with a big group of other parents and children. "What are we waiting for?" he huffed. "It's very draughty in here."

"It's a tour of the school," said Ingrid patiently. "It was on the schedule I sent you."

"Well, it was supposed to start seven minutes ago, so I assumed it had been cancelled," Ingrid's dad grumbled, looking at his watch. Ingrid rolled her eyes.

Luckily Pym and Luigi turned up at that moment. The rest of my family were off working on their top secret plan, plus we had decided that including everyone on a school tour could have led to difficulties.

"Pym!" I said, happily. "And Luigi! These are Ingrid's parents."

"So lovely to see you again!" Ingrid's mum beamed at Luigi.

"Oh, and you!" exclaimed Luigi. "How have you been?"

"Fine, fine," said Ingrid's mum, still smiling.

"Sorry, have you two met?" asked Pym.

"No," said Ingrid shortly.

"Really?" said Luigi, baffled. "How extraordinary. I could have sworn you were the Princess of Baronthorn."

There was a pause. "You thought Ingrid's mum was the Princess of Baronthorn?" I asked.

"Who?" asked Luigi.

"Ingrid's mum," I said, pointing at her. "Mrs Blammel."

"Delighted to meet you." Luigi swept into a little bow. It was my turn to roll my eyes then.

"Ahem." A cough interrupted us. Turning towards the staircase we spotted Mr Grant standing on the third stair up. "If you'd all like to follow me, the tour is about to begin." We all grinned then, because a tour with Mr Grant was bound to be interesting.

Everyone fell in behind him as he started guiding us up the staircase. "So, I'm going to show you around some of our classrooms," he was saying with a smile. "That way you can see where it is that your children spend their time having fun ... and learning of course!" He laughed, and all the women (and some of the men) in the group joined in a bit too loudly, their moony eyes glued to Mr Grant's handsome face. "Now, this is an interesting piece of school history." Mr Grant came to a halt on the second bend in the staircase in front of a large painting. "This stunning piece of art used to hang in the great hall, and it's a portrait of the final owner of Saint Smithen's before it became a school: Lord Phineas Scrimshaw."

I gasped and next to me I felt Kip and Ingrid stiffen. Phineas Scrimshaw? I looked at the painting and gasped again. I had seen it before. It was the portrait that Maxwell Dangerfield had taken such a fancy to. To think that we had actually been looking at the face of Phineas Scrimshaw every day on our way to lessons! It suddenly struck me that Phineas Scrimshaw had been a real person who ate and slept and laughed and lived right here, who had walked up and down these exact stairs two hundred years ago. It made me feel a bit shivery, but I also finally understood why Miss Baxter had given me the assignment to research the school. Looking at all the paintings that crowded the wall, I felt like I was seeing them for the first time. I realized that each one was a story connected to the building's history. It felt funny to think that I was part of that history now as well.

"Of course Lord Scrimshaw was also something

of an explorer in his youth, and he was a great collector," Mr Grant continued.

Ingrid's dad perked up. "A collector? A collector of what exactly? Did he collect ... stamps?" he squeaked urgently.

Ingrid buried her head in her hands and Mr Grant looked surprised. "Er no, not stamps," he said apologetically. "Natural history samples. Fossils mostly."

"Oh, well, I'm hardly interested in a load of old bones," Ingrid's dad huffed. "Nowhere near as interesting as stamps."

Something was tugging at the corner of my brain like a squirrel at an obstinate acorn. But it flew out of my head straight away, because in the crowd I spotted something much more significant. Or should that be *someone*. I nudged Pym's shoulder and nodded my head. She turned slightly in that direction and then gave me the thumbs up. We had spotted Lucas Quest, and it was time to put our plan into action.

CHAPTER TWENTY-EIGHT

Standing in the entrance hall, surrounded by other chattering families, Lucas Quest seemed to have deserted his own family and was standing with Annabelle and her parents. Annabelle's parents were as terrible as you might expect. Her dad looked like a big pink bulldog with a bristling moustache. Her mum was dressed from head to toe in pale pink. A pale pink skirt and jacket, shiny pale pink shoes and a shiny pale pink bag. The only things that weren't pale pink were her blonde hair, which was piled on top of her head, and her little blue eyes which were cold and mean, just like Annabelle's.

Lucas was busy sucking up to Annabelle's parents, his movie-star smile turned up to "eye-wateringly blinding", and Annabelle's mum was eating it up, giggling girlishly at whatever he was saying. Normally they wouldn't have looked twice at us, but Pym and I had a secret weapon – Luigi. Mr and Mrs Forthington-Smythe, like most terrible snobs, were very aware that Luigi was actually a Lord, and the fourteenth Earl of Burnshire. In fact they were distant acquaintances of Luigi's old battleaxe of an aunt, Hortence.

I looked at Luigi and touched the side of my nose, which was the secret signal to put the plan into action. Luigi gave me a very deep and meaningful nod and slipped over to Annabelle's family.

"Well, if it isn't the Forthington-Smythes," Luigi exclaimed, clapping Annabelle's dad on the shoulder.

"Your Lordship!" fluttered Annabelle's mother. "How splendid to see you. I do so hope your aunt is keeping well."

"Old Hortence?" Luigi asked. "Should think so, old dragon that she is. She'll outlive us all!" and he snorted with noisy laughter. Then he caught my eye and I shook my head sharply. Luigi's laughter died instantly. "Ahem," he said. "Sorry. I mean her ladyship is tolerably well and would, I'm sure, wish for me to pass on her very best wishes." And he bowed low over Mrs Forthington-Smythe's hand, leaving her all aflutter.

"Capital, capital." Mr Forthington-Smythe slapped Luigi so heartily on the back that he was left wincing and breathless.

Annabelle was watching this conversation with narrowed eyes. She was obviously not fooled by Luigi's nice act. "I think your group might be leaving without you," she said sharply, her eyes flicking in my direction. I pretended to be totally absorbed by a painting of a cockerel on the wall.

"Annabelle!" her mother snapped. "Don't be so rude! Forgive her, your Lordship. And might I introduce Annabelle's friend, Lucas Quest. You might recognize him."

"You aren't related to the Princess of Baronthorn, are you?" Luigi looked at Lucas suspiciously.

"Not that I know of," Lucas twinkled.

"Dashed if I can work out what she has to do with anything." Luigi scratched his head.

"Er, no. I mean, yes," Lucas agreed uncertainly, flashing that mega-watt smile again.

Mrs Forthington-Smythe looked ready to burst at this casual mention of royalty. "Lucas is something of a film star," she gushed.

"Oh, right," said Luigi. "Don't go in for the motion pictures much myself, but jolly good for you." I shot him a look that said it was time to hurry things along. "Anyway," said Luigi, "this tour's not quite the ticket, eh? Used to be a Saint Smithen's boy myself, you know; could do a much better job. Tell you all the real stories. Shall I show you around?"

Mrs Forthington-Smythe looked ready to expire with joy at this, and Mr Forthington-Smythe let out a booming laugh. "Capital, capital," he repeated, clapping a wincing Luigi on the back once more.

"Well, if you follow me through here. . ." Luigi croaked, guiding the party down the stairs.

"It's time!" I whispered to Kip, Ingrid and Pym.

"Mum, Dad, I have to go," Ingrid said to her parents. Her dad was deep in conversation with a kindred spirit about stamps and didn't even look up.

"Have fun, darling," her mum said placidly, and Ingrid kissed her on the cheek before we whisked off, back down the stairs.

Outside the great hall we met Inspector Hartley, waiting with curiosity burning in his eyes. "Well, Miss Pym," he said, "do you want to tell me what this note is about, telling me to meet you here?" He

215

held up a piece of paper. "Or why I've just watched your lion-tamer friend hustle a group of people inside the hall while giving me an enormous wink?"

"All will become clear in just a moment, Inspector. If you will just step inside..."

I held the door open and all of us except Pym crept into the back of the great hall. Luigi had moved his group to the front near the stage, and they had their backs to us. I looked at the windows and was relieved to see all the curtains were closed. Reaching up to the wall, I hit the light switch and the room was plunged into darkness.

"What the devil?" I heard Mr Forthington-Smythe curse, and then a sharp intake of breath from the inspector, followed by blood-curdling screams from Annabelle and her mother.

Because there, standing on the stage, glowing and transparent, was a ghost.

CHAPTER TWENTY-NINE

The ghost seemed to glow and shimmer. His whole body was made of a curious green light and his feet floated inches above the ground. He was wearing old-fashioned armour and had flowing robes tied around his shoulders. His ferocious face was battle-scarred and his eyes held a murderous rage. He was also holding a particularly deadly looking dagger.

"SILENCE!" the ghost roared, cutting through the terrified screams.

"Wh-who are you?" Mr Forthington-Smythe stuttered.

"I am the original King Duncan, first victim of the curse of the Scottish Play. Murdered by this very dagger." The ghost held the dagger in the air and plunged it down in front of him. "And I am here to question someone in this room. Someone in this room who has LIED and CHEATED. Someone in this room who is a DASTARDLY CRIMINAL."

"Now, look here, you can't just—" Mr Forthington-Smythe's blustering was cut short by the ghost's terrible shouts.

"I said *silence*! I am not talking to you, but to another. HE KNOWS WHO HE IS."

A gasp of fear reached my ears.

"Lucas Quest!" the ghost boomed.

A terrified whimper in the dark confirmed Lucas's presence.

"W-what do you w-want?" Lucas gasped.

"I want JUSTICE!" The ghost's voice echoed around the room.

"Justice?" Lucas repeated, weakly.

"Yes." The ghost nodded. "I know what others do not. I know what you are. I know what you have done!"

Lucas whimpered again.

"Lucas?" Annabelle's voice was shrill. "What is that . . . that *thing* talking about? What is going on?"

"I d-d-don't know," stuttered Lucas.

"LIAR!" The ground seemed to tremble as the

voice rumbled through the air. "You are a liar, Lucas Quest, and it is time to confess to your crimes."

"I don't know what you're talking about," Lucas whispered again.

"I think you do know," the ghost shouted, and he lifted the dagger in his hand again. "Do I have to *make* you talk?"

"No, no," cried Lucas, "I'll talk, I'll talk. I'll tell you everything! Please don't hurt me!" He sounded close to tears.

"Very well." The ghost lowered the dagger slightly. "Enlighten us."

"I-I wanted the part of Macbeth," Lucas whispered.

"Speak up!" boomed the ghost. "We can't hear you."

"I wanted the part of Macbeth," Lucas repeated, "so I . . . I sabotaged the play."

"What did you do?" asked the ghost mercilessly. "Tell me everything."

"I painted that warning on the sheet," gasped Lucas, "and I hung it across the stage."

"What else?" the ghost demanded.

"I put some medicine in Gary's sandwich. Something to make him sick."

"And?"

"And I cut the rope holding up the chandelier so that it would fall on Maxwell." Lucas's voice was now barely above a whisper.

"And?"

"And what?" Lucas cried. "That's everything, I swear!"

The ghost laughed humourlessly "I don't think so, Lucas. Tell me about the fire."

"The fire?" Lucas's voice faltered. "The fire at the town hall? You think I had something to do with that? I didn't! I didn't!" His voice was starting to sound hysterical.

The ghost looked confused. "Er, sorry. What?"

I was confused, too. Lucas sounded like he was telling the truth, but I was so certain he was behind everything.

"I didn't start the fire!" Lucas screeched. "I swear it! It was just when all the reporters turned up and talking about the curse, that gave me the idea. If we could get even more media attention then the play would have a big audience. That meant I needed a starring role. Then when the fire scared off some of the actors I thought maybe I could, you know ... scare off a few more somehow. Or they could meet with little accidents and everyone would blame the curse."

"Oh. Right ... um..." the ghost floundered a little. With a sudden scuffling noise he disappeared and a split second later another ghost appeared. This time it was a hideous crone.

"Aaaaaaaaaagh!" wailed Lucas.

The ghost looked pleased. "Bah!" she cried. "Yes, it is me." She pointed a finger at Lucas. "You tell me truth or I curse you! I curse you very, very bad."

"But I *am* telling you the truth!" Lucas exclaimed. "I admit I did those other things, but I didn't start the fire! I wasn't anywhere near the second floor. I had been arguing with Maxwell about my part and I ran outside. You can ask him, ask Maxwell. I didn't do it!" Lucas blubbered. "The Love Vampire film just got all those mean reviews and I needed people to take me seriously. They've even cancelled the second film. Just when I was about to have my big break! How will people know how amazing I am? This was my chance to show everyone. I'm a great actor!" he screeched, "I'm the best one! I ought to be a star!"

With that the lights flicked back on and I turned and saw Inspector Hartley standing beside the switches. "I think I've heard enough," he said. "Young man, you're going to have to come with me and answer some questions about this sabotage of yours. Not to mention the charges of bodily harm."

Lucas, Annabelle and her parents were all standing, pale and silent, their mouths hanging open.

"W-w-what?" Lucas gasped.

"Poisoning and attempted assault with a chandelier, wasn't it?" The inspector raised an eyebrow and looked at his notebook. How had he even managed to make notes in the dark? I was seriously impressed.

"That is it?" the ghost on stage asked sullenly with a stomp of her foot. "I didn't even get to do my best bit." The ghost ran her finger across her throat and shouted, "I KEEL YOU, DEAD!" in a very dramatic way.

"Sorry," said the inspector, trying not to laugh. "You were both very frightening."

The old crone was bustled away and replaced by the original ghost. "Thank you," he said, looking pleased. "Although I do think we should have changed my character's name. What do you think of King Boris?"

"You!" hissed Annabelle, her face pale and her icy eyes boring in to mine. "I should have known you'd find a way to ruin everything."

"It's not Poppy's fault your boyfriend is a psycho," pointed out Kip, helpfully.

"I think you're perfect together," Ingrid said to Annabelle with her sweetest smile.

"Just watch your back," Annabelle spat, jabbing her finger in my direction. "I'll make sure everyone sees you for what you really are – a nasty, nosy weirdo who doesn't belong here." With that she swept towards the door, her nose in the air and her blonde ponytail bouncing. Inspector Hartley hustled Lucas and the Forthington-Smythes out behind her and Pym popped her head around the door.

"How did it go?" she asked.

"It went perfectly," I said, "apart from one tiny problem. I believed him. Lucas didn't start the fire."

CHAPTER THIRTY

"Are you sure?" Pym asked, surprised.

"Yes." Ingrid nodded. "He confessed to the rest but not to the fire. He didn't do it."

"And if he had, he would have admitted it." Kip chuckled. "He was so scared; I thought he was going to wet himself."

"That's funny," said Ingrid, "because someone was sitting next to me making funny, squeaking noises and digging his fingernails into my arm."

"I just didn't want you to feel bad if you were scared," said Kip breezily. "It was very realistic, you know, so I could understand that you might be fooled."

"So I guess the fire must have been an accident,

after all," I said slowly. "I really thought Lucas had done it all, but he was just taking advantage of the fire and all the talk of the curse to get people to drop out of the play."

"But that's good news," said Pym after a pause. "You still got the saboteur. I could hear lots of shrieking through the door but I just told people that a rehearsal was taking place."

"It was BRILLIANT," Kip said, solemnly.

"How did you do it?" Ingrid asked, pushing her glasses up her nose. "I don't blame Lucas for being scared – it was incredibly believable."

Marvin appeared from the side of the stage. "It's called Pepper's Ghost." He grinned.

"Of course," breathed Ingrid. "Genius!"

"Pepper's Ghost?" asked Kip.

"A trick named after John Henry Pepper," said Ingrid. "He famously performed it in 1862."

"But how does it work?" Kip sounded intrigued.

Marvin walked further forward on to the stage and then, suddenly stopping, reached out and tapped on something. Only then, looking really closely, could you see that there was actually a big sheet of glass on the stage set at an odd angle.

"It works just like a mirror," Marvin continued,

smiling down at his captive audience. "Here in the wings we dress up an actor as a ghost and shine a light on him so that he—"

"Or she!" a voice interrupted from the wings. "Ghosts can be girls too!"

"Very right, very right. So that he *or she* will appear to glow. The actor is reflected in the glass, and when the glass is moved around at an angle, then the reflection is seen by the audience. Only because the glass is see-through and invisible from down there, a transparent glowing ghost appears to be standing in the middle of the stage!"

Fanella and Boris bustled out in their costumes. "It is us all along," Fanella cried jubilantly. "We trick everyone! And I was so scary!"

"Not as scary as me," muttered Boris.

"WHAT IS THAT YOU ARE SAYING?" Fanella turned on him.

"You were both very scary," I said. "It was brilliant. And we might have been wrong about the fire, but we did catch the saboteur, so that's the main thing, I suppose."

At that moment Ingrid's parents stuck their heads around the door. "Ah, Ingrid, there you are," said her dad. "There's time for a quick tea break before we go back to the hotel to get ready for the big Halloween party this evening. Are you coming?"

"Tea?" Kip's head whipped around. "Is there cake?"

Mr Blammel looked surprised. "Um, I think there were some biscuits," he said.

"Biscuits?!" Kip wrinkled his nose. "Well, I suppose that will have to do, but come on, everyone, let's hustle or all the chocolate ones will be gone," and he tore out towards the dining hall, quickly followed by the others.

I hung back with Pym. "Now, Poppy," she said, "there's something else going on with you, isn't there? Something's wrong. Do you want to talk to me about it?"

This was the moment I had been waiting for, and I knew it was time to ask the questions that felt like they were taking up more and more room in my brain every day. My stomach did an impressive somersault. "Er, yes. I think so. Yes," I stuttered.

Pym smiled at me expectantly. My heart was skittering like a hyperactive kangaroo and I reached for the right words.

Then I reached for *any* words.

"Well, the thing is," I began, rubbing my sweating

palms on my school skirt, "the *thing*, well … the thing *is*…"

"Yes, love," said Pym. "What is the thing?"

"It's about Parents' Weekend," I blurted. Pym's smile dimmed a little, but she nodded encouragingly. "I suppose it made me think about my parents," I continued. "My real parents, I mean. Not that you're not my real parent, Pym!" I gasped. I was doing this all wrong. It was like my brain and my mouth weren't connected.

My brain was yelling. *Say something! Tell Pym you love her and you're scared and you don't want to hurt her feelings, but you need some answers. Did your parents really not want you? Why? What's wrong with you? Why did they leave you behind?*

My mouth said, "I – I… The… I mean, my… What I…"

Then my brain said, *Nice one, Poppy. Great job!* (My brain can be a bit sarcastic when it wants to be.)

Pym squeezed my hand gently. "You want to know more about your birth parents?" she asked, smiling a small smile that didn't quite reach her eyes. I nodded gratefully. "Well," she said, taking a deep breath, "I don't know very much, but I do have—"

228

But I didn't find out what Pym was going to say just then because we were interrupted by Letty blasting through the doors. "There you are, Poppy!" she yelped. "I've been looking for you everywhere. We've got to get ready for the Halloween party ... you know getting into my costume is a three-person job." She trailed off as she caught sight of our faces. "Sorry! Am I interrupting?"

"No, no!" I exclaimed brightly. "We were just... I mean..."

"Poppy and I can finish this conversation later." Pym squeezed my hand again and I returned the squeeze, gratefully. "I think I have something that may help," she whispered in my ear. "I'll give it to you tomorrow morning. Meet me at the tent, early." Then she turned to face Letty. "Now you two run along, I want to see you looking really gruesome!"

CHAPTER THIRTY-ONE

Anyone walking past our dorm room would think they were witnesses at the site of a gory crime scene. There were severed limbs on the floor, a bottle of fake blood had been knocked over and was drip-drip-dripping sinisterly from one of the nightstands. On one of the beds a chalk-white ghost sat in a blood-spattered nightgown, her nose firmly in a book. I was trying to help pin another leg on to the giant spider in front of me. "Is it even?" Letty asked, waggling the other legs in Ingrid's direction.

Ingrid looked up. "That one on the right needs to go up a bit."

Letty spun around, knocking more things off

the nightstand with her extra legs. "Oops!" she exclaimed. "I'll have to be careful with this tonight!"

"They look really good, Letty," I said admiringly. "How did you make them?"

"Filled all my black tights with newspaper." Letty swung around, taking down a precariously balanced pile of books.

Once the final leg had been pinned on I turned to my own reflection in the mirror. Even though I was a bit disappointed we hadn't uncovered a terrible arsonist, I was glad that now I could focus on Halloween and having a great party with my pals. Plus, I had to admit I looked pretty excellent. Letty had sprayed my hair with wash-out green dye, and I pulled my pointy witches' hat down over the top of it before adjusting my warty nose. "I'm a bit worried about these," I said, lifting my arms and turning towards Letty, showing off the long sleeves on my black dress. "What if they get in the way?"

Letty nodded. "Yes, you do need to be careful to take these things into account when designing a costume. Nothing worse than bits that get in the way." She bent down to tie her shoes and hit me in the face with a newspaper-stuffed leg. "Right!" she chirped. "We all look great! Let's go!"

231

We made our way over to the great hall, joining the noisy stream of zombies and vampires also heading that way. The driveway was lined with carved pumpkins containing flickering candles and as we made our way through to the entrance hall I was delighted to see that the ceiling was thick with cobwebs and rubber bats dangling on strings. Students and parents milled around in brilliant costumes and the room was full of chatter. I spotted pirates, fairies, superheroes and even two people dressed up as a pantomime horse. ("I feel sorry for the person who has to be a horse's bum all night!" Letty whispered.) In the great hall more candles were lit in the candelabras along the walls. Masked waiters in uniforms were moving through the room with little bits of fancy food on round trays, and a long table ran almost the entire length of the hall, laden with plates full of Halloween goodies. There were cupcakes topped with swirls of orange icing, sandwiches cut into the shape of tombstones that stood on plates of leafy green salad, bowls of jelly worms, trays of toffee apples, and round biscuits iced to look like eyeballs. In the middle of the table a large black cauldron full of hot punch stood, clouds of steam tumbling out of the top. Unsurprisingly we found Kip by the food. A large plastic knife seemed to be sticking through his head, his clothes were ripped and covered in blood and his face was painted green. He was holding a paper plate piled high with treats and was trying to balance another biscuit on top of the already swaying tower.

"Hi, guys!" he mumbled, clearly focused on the task in front of him.

"Everything looks amazing!" I exclaimed, helping myself to a chocolate finger.

"Ooh! There's Greg, I wanted to talk to him about the staging for Monday!" Letty exclaimed and she ran off, knocking several cups of punch over with her spider legs on the way.

"Hello, children!" a voice came from behind us. I turned around to find myself face to face with Penny Farthing, who was dressed as a giant black cat.

"Penny!" I exclaimed. "What are you doing here?"

"Miss Baxter was kind enough to invite all of the Brimwell Players along," Penny sang. "I must say after all the drama I'll be glad when the performance is finished on Monday, but it is lovely being in this beautiful building."

A waiter wearing a rubber gorilla mask

interrupted us, swooping a large silver tray under our noses. "Anyone for mini chocolate cakes?" he asked in a muffled voice.

"CAKE?" Kip's voice squeaked, and he stuffed one straight in his mouth before adding as many as he could to the pile on his plate.

"There aren't any peanuts in them, are there, dear?" Penny asked the waiter. "I'm deathly allergic, you know. Such a pain."

"No madam, no peanuts," the waiter replied, bowing forward a little at the waist as though Penny was a super fancy lady.

"Ooh, well … maybe just one then!" Penny fluttered at him and picked the last cake off the tray.

"Better go and re-stock!" the waiter's muffled voice came from behind his mask and he headed back out of the room.

"I know I shouldn't, but I really can't resist chocolate cake!" Penny twinkled, raising the tempting pud to her lips.

"NOOOOOOOOOOOOOOOO!" screamed Kip, and it was as if the world went into slow motion as he hurled himself through the air and knocked Penny to the ground. He wrestled the cake from her hand and smushed it into his own greedy mouth.

234

Ingrid and I were staring down at the pair of them, sprawled on the floor, our mouths hanging wide open like the most gormless of goldfishes. The room was silent and Miss Baxter appeared at our sides, reaching down to help Penny up.

"Miss Farthing, are you all right?" she asked in a worried voice. "What on earth happened?"

"This young man . . . knocked me over . . . and . . . stole my cake!" Penny burst into tears.

"Kip!" Miss Baxter exclaimed. "Is this true?!"

"Yes," Kip spoke, spitting cake crumbs everywhere. "But it's not what you think!" He turned to Penny. "There *are* peanuts in them."

"What?!" Miss Baxter sounded flummoxed.

"I knew as soon as I tasted the first one. The cakes have peanut butter in 'em. And she's allergic." Kip nodded his head in Penny's direction. "She told the waiter."

"But Kip, why did you eat the cake?" I asked.

Kip looked puzzled. "What else was I going to do with it?"

"He's right about the cake," someone piped up from the crowd, and I noticed Miss Marigold was there dressed as a pirate. "It's my chocolate peanut butter fudge cake. Made them myself."

"My DEAR BOY!" Penny grabbed Kip and hugged him tightly to her chest. "You have SAVED MY LIFE! HOW shall I ever repay you?!"

Miss Baxter tugged gently on Penny's arm, causing her to release a Kip whose red face was showing through the green face paint. "Let's get you a drink, Miss Farthing. You must be quite shaken. I'm so sorry that such a mistake was made. Thank goodness for such a quick thinker." She smiled at Kip who turned even redder.

"Thank goodness Kip scoffs everything straight away and knows the difference between every kind of cake, you mean!" I said, punching him lightly on the arm.

Penny and Miss Baxter melted into the crowd and everyone had gone back to their conversations.

"Well, that was weird," I said quietly, as Kip and Ingrid huddled towards me.

"Yes," Ingrid said, pushing her glasses up her nose. "That waiter specifically said there were no peanuts in the cakes."

"So?" Kip shrugged. "He must have made a mistake."

"There have been an awful lot of mistakes and accidents recently," I murmured.

"Do you think this has something to do with the other accidents?" Ingrid asked in a whisper.

"I thought the mystery was solved!" Kip groaned. "We already know that Lucas was sabotaging the play."

"Yes," I nodded, "but we never found out who started the fire."

"But wasn't that just an accident?" Kip murmured.

"Dougie Valentine always says there ARE no accidents!" I exclaimed. "Something else is going on here – something BIG."

"So what do you want to do next?" Ingrid asked, turning her huge eyes on me.

"I think we should find that waiter," I said. "Ask him some questions."

We looked all around the room but even though I spotted waiters in zombie masks and witch masks and werewolf masks I couldn't find a man in a gorilla mask anywhere. We moved out into the entrance hall but he wasn't there either. Finally, we stumbled outside just to make sure no one was out there.

"I don't understand!" Kip frowned. "He's disappeared."

"I'm not so sure about that," I said, bending

down next to one of the pumpkin lanterns where something lay on the ground. I picked it up and held it in the light.

In my hands was a rubber gorilla mask.

"He's gone," said Kip.

"But who *was* he?" asked Ingrid.

"What's this?" I muttered, picking up a scrumpled piece of paper from next to the mask. Ingrid pulled a torch out of her pocket and I unfolded the paper and held it up to the light.

Then we all gasped.

CHAPTER THIRTY-TWO

"Is that what I think it is?" asked Kip, breaking the eerie silence that had fallen over us.

"It is," I said. "But . . . how?"

"The second clue!" breathed Ingrid.

And it looked as if she was right because the yellowing piece of paper that I held in my hand looked a lot like the second of the three riddles that led to Scrimshaw's gold.

Riddle me two, an easier clue,
If you know oak from ash and yew.
The thirteenth which from acorns grow
'Neath aged trunk there dig below.

"Is it real?" asked Kip.

"Only one way to find out!" I said. "We'd better solve it."

We all read over it again. "It seems to be saying that it's buried under the thirteenth oak tree," mused Ingrid. "But the thirteenth from where?"

"It's not very helpful, is it?" Kip muttered.

"Well, we know he didn't want to make things too easy," I said, looking out at all the ancient oaks that towered in front of Saint Smithen's. "I bet he thought it would be really funny having all his horrible family digging under all these oak trees."

"But it might not even be at St Smithen's," Kip pointed out. "It doesn't mention the building in the clue."

"I'm sure it's here," I said firmly, with more confidence than I felt. "It's worth a look, anyway."

"But where do we start?" asked Kip.

Ingrid was still frowning over the clue. "It could be something to do with the acorn," she said. "I mean, oak trees grow from acorns, but it could also be read as the thirteenth FROM the acorns."

We all racked our brains and I felt an imaginary light bulb PING in my brain.

"I know where it is!" I exclaimed. "The starting

point . . . it's the sundial!"

"Of course!" Ingrid's eyes glowed behind her glasses.

"What sundial?" asked Kip.

"The one further down the drive," I said, already hurrying in that direction, Ingrid right beside me shining her torch in front of us. Kip scurried close behind.

When we reached the sundial, I pointed to the top, and Ingrid held her torch up so that we could all get a good look. "You see!" I breathed. "All the acorns are engraved in the design here."

"And what's this?" Ingrid was bending down and brushing moss away from the sundial's base. The words ERECTED BY P.SCRIMSHAW, 1820 were carved into the stone.

"THIS IS IT!" yelled Kip.

"Sssssshhhhhhh!" Ingrid and I hissed.

"We don't want to draw any attention, Kip! We need to be stealthy," I whispered.

Kip nodded a very serious nod and crouched down to the floor.

"What are you doing?" I asked.

"Stealth mode . . . initiated," was Kip's reply.

Ingrid and I exchanged a look.

"OK, so thirteen oak trees from here... It could be in that direction." I pointed right. "Or that one." I pointed straight ahead.

"Let's try straight ahead first," whispered Ingrid.

We set off, Kip rolling and tumbling along the floor, humming his own theme tune under his breath, and Ingrid and I counting trees.

"Eleven ... twelve ... thirteen!" I counted aloud. "I wonder if this is the right one?"

"I don't suppose there's much we can do without getting a spade," said Ingrid, shivering. "I guess we should have thought of that."

"Yes," I agreed, frustration filling my voice. "What sort of treasure seekers are we?"

"You guys..." Kip's voice came from the other side of the tree, and his face popped around the side. "I'm pretty sure this is the right place."

"What makes you say that?" I asked walking around to where he was standing.

"Well ... that big hole with the spade in was my first clue," Kip said, pointing to them.

Ingrid and I boggled. There, at the bottom of the tree, was a hole about three feet deep. The abandoned spade made it clear that someone had found what they were looking for and disappeared in a hurry. They hadn't even bothered to fill in the hole, although there was a thick layer of soggy autumn leaves in the bottom of it.

"Whoever dug here must have done it days ago," I said heavily, pointing to the leaves. I couldn't believe that someone had solved the clue and beaten us to it! More importantly they had taken the third clue, and without that there was no hope of us completing our treasure hunt.

Then Ingrid asked the question that was weighing on everyone's minds.

"But ... who else is looking for Scrimshaw's gold?"

CHAPTER THIRTY-THREE

We racked our brains all evening in search of the answer to who else could be on the hunt for Phineas Scrimshaw's lost gold, but we were stumped. The next morning we were no closer to having an answer. Unfortunately there was not a lot left for us to do when our investigation had hit such a dead end. We had no idea who had dropped the clue or dug the hole, and my brain was absolutely full of questions wriggling all over each other, like piglets at a trough of tasty slop.

It was day two of Parents' Weekend and I was up super early. Not only did I have a hidden treasure to locate, but I had an appointment with Pym that I definitely didn't want to miss. I wandered down to the dip in the school grounds where the circus had set up the big top tent and their trailers, ready for my first bit of trapeze practice in weeks. My stomach was skittering with anticipation and nerves, wondering what it was that Pym was going to give me, and how it related to the mystery of my parents.

When Pym arrived I was already hanging with my legs hooked over the trapeze, and it felt wonderful to soar back and forth in a wide, swooping arc. Pym clambered up on to the trapeze opposite me and held out her hands.

"Come across!" she called, and I threw myself forward, tumbling through the air and reaching for Pym's hand.

In a flash I was back in my dream, and for a moment I hesitated, my hand not quite reaching out far enough. That was all it took. Missing Pym's fingers by millimetres I found myself falling through the air and hitting the safety net with a terrific bounce.

"Rats!" I wheezed, feeling the air rush out of me like a popped balloon.

"Needs some work..." Pym's voice floated down to me.

With a groan I heaved myself out of the net and perched on the edge, dusting off my purple tie-dyed leggings on the way.

"You're just a bit out of practice," Pym said quietly when she had climbed down and reached my side.

I put my hands on my knees and squinted up at the empty trapeze swaying above. "I know," I grumbled. "What sort of school doesn't have a flying trapeze? I mean, you can't move for TEXT BOOKS," I huffed. "And if you want to play netball they can't do enough for you. Nets, balls, they've got it all. But you make one tiiiiny suggestion that they build a nice, simple trapeze and they LAUGH at you like you're JOKING." I threw my arms in the air.

"I thought you liked being at Saint Smithen's?" Pym asked gently, her bad eye scrunched up in my direction and watching me carefully.

"I do," I said with a sigh. "But I miss the circus, and you, and all of this –" I looked around me, taking it all in. "I just feel like I understand things better when I'm with you. I understand who I am. But when I'm here by myself it's just a bit ... different." I rubbed my nose, puzzling over the churned-up feelings that were swirling away inside me.

After a thoughtful pause Pym piped up. "Well, I think that's a good thing, love. It's good to see lots of different things and go to different places. To think about what makes you, you, and where you come from." She looked around the big top with a grin.

"Where I come from —" I frowned.

"Yes," Pym smiled that smile again, the one that didn't quite reach her eyes. "I always knew that you would ask me about your parents one day, and that it wouldn't be easy. . ." she squeezed my hand, ". . . for either of us."

I started to say something, but Pym held up her hand. "This is for you," she said solemnly, reaching into her pocket and handing me a brown envelope. I opened it and shook the contents out into my hand. A blank sealed envelope, and a battered receipt fell out. I looked up at Pym. "That's not all," she said, reaching into her pocket. I gasped as she pulled out a beautiful silver necklace. She laid it in the palm of my other hand, and I stared at the little silver heart on the delicate chain, feeling the tug of familiarity. Had this belonged to my mother?

"I'm not sure if this holds any of the answers you are looking for," Pym murmured. "But these are the things that you had with you when you arrived at the circus. If you do want to know more about your parents, this is a good place to start."

My mouth opened, ready for the thousands of questions I had inside me to come spilling out, but

247

instead I was distracted by a terrible wailing noise.

Pym's body tensed. "Oh dear, is that BoBo?"

"Neeeeee-naaaaaaaaa, neeeeee-naaaaa." BoBo sounded like a disaster siren as she raced towards us at full speed, the rest of her body struggling to keep up with her short legs. "Pym! EMEEEERGENCY!!!!" she screeched, tumbling over herself and rolling across the floor. She came to an untidy stop below my feet. I swiftly pressed the necklace and envelope into Pym's hand and she slipped them back in her

248

pocket. I think she knew that I just wasn't ready to share them with anyone but her just yet.

"What's wrong?" I asked as I helped BoBo up.

"Marvin … guinea pigs … won't … stop…" BoBo panted, running outside and pointing back the way she came, towards the school. Pym and I both groaned and ran over as fast as we could.

As we approached the main school building it was clear that things had gone very wrong. Sounds of smashing and shouting drifted out of the open door. We were almost knocked down by two ladies who were presumably parents, scuttling past us. They were wide-eyed and trembling. "The guinea pigs…" one lady croaked in a haunted whisper.

Inside the dining hall, instead of a few early risers munching some breakfast, what we saw was a disaster zone. Furniture was tumbled everywhere. Chuckles was standing on top of a chair miming breathing into a paper bag, and Sharp-Eye Sheila and Boris were cowering in one corner. Boris was holding a broom out in front of him with shaking hands, while a cluster of parents huddled behind him.

"Stay back!" he boomed.

Fanella was standing on top of one of the dining tables.

"MARVIN, YOU GET THESE RODENTS GONE OR I LET OTIS LOOSE RIGHT NOW!" she shrieked. It was then that I noticed the whole floor seemed to be moving, or more precisely, wriggling.

"Are those—" I began.

"Guinea pigs," Pym agreed flatly. "Hundreds of the things."

In the corner of the room I spotted Marvin and Doris huddled over a gleaming black top hat, which was spilling over with an ever-growing number of wide-eyed, snuffley guinea pigs. Marvin was desperately thrusting guinea pigs back in the hat. "Abracadabra! ABRACADABRA!" His shouts were increasingly shrill and panicked.

"I don't think Abracadabera's going to cut it this time," Doris huffed. "Where's the off switch? I told you we needed a safety measure. Where are my blueprints?"

"I keel you, Marvin," Fanella screeched, dragging a finger across her throat, threateningly. "I keel you dead. This is *worse* than octopus. And you *know* that octopus is steal my earrings!"

Marvin jerked up, guinea pigs tumbling merrily from his hands. "You and I both know there WERE NO EARRINGS!" he yelled, his face a deep, beetrooty red. "And that was ONE TIME!" His protests were drowned out by another wave of cheery, squeaking guinea pigs.

"You might want to have a look at that hat, Doris," Pym said.

Doris nodded briskly and pushed her glasses up her nose. "Problems with the regulator," she said thoughtfully. "Need to do some calculations. One guinea pig is probably enough."

"Bah! One of these terrible guinea piglets is more than enough," Fanella grumbled. "Me, I never want to see a guinea piglet never AGAIN. One more thing goes wrong before my big performance and I keel you, Marvin! This time I mean it! I keel you and I bury your bones in the ground and then I dance on them. I DANCE ON THEM!"

"I say, Fanella," said Luigi, squeamishly, "I think that's a bit much."

But I didn't hear anything else because my brain was whirring away at an alarming rate.

"Bury your bones ... bones ... bones ..." I muttered. Something was gnawing away at me, like a guinea pig on a bourbon biscuit. Suddenly the thing that was nagging at my brain became as clear in my mind as the scene before me. I needed to talk to Kip and Ingrid. Right away.

CHAPTER THIRTY-FOUR

I left my family to battle with the guinea pigs because I was filled with a sense of extraordinary purpose and keen detective instincts. Now the game was well and truly afoot!

Fortunately I didn't have to use up any of those detective instincts on tracking down Kip and Ingrid because at that very moment they were walking over the gravel path towards me.

"Kip! Ingrid!" I cried urgently, "I need to talk to you ... RIGHT NOW!"

"Does it have to be right now, Poppy?" Kip groaned. "It *is* breakfast time after all."

"Trust me." I spoke in a hushed voice. "What I

have to say is SO HUGE that you won't even care about breakfast."

Kip and Ingrid looked at me with awed expressions on their faces. That was big talk. I led them further down the drive and away from all the squeaking and crashing that was still coming from the dining room. We reached one of the comfortable oak trees and huddled underneath its red and orange parasol.

"What is it? What's going on, Poppy?" Kip asked, looking into my face. "You're bright red."

"I think I have an idea about Scrimshaw's gold," I said, and it was like I had electrified them both.

"W-what?" said Kip. "You know where the gold is?"

"No," I said, "but I think I've worked out the first clue!"

"That's amazing!" said Ingrid. "I've been trying to work it out all night. I think I was even dreaming about it. What is it?"

"Well," I said, "remember what Penny said, about Scrimshaw being a collector?"

"Yeah," Kip nodded.

"Mr Grant said the same thing, about all Scrimshaw's fossils," Ingrid said, thoughtfully.

"Yes," I agreed quickly, "and then Ingrid, your dad said he wasn't interested in a *load of old bones*!"

Realization was spreading over Kip and Ingrid's faces.

"You don't mean. . ." Kip trailed off.

"Set a fire beneath my bones," Ingrid breathed. "He meant his *collection* of bones?"

"I think so," I said seriously, "but, wait, that's not all."

The seriousness of my voice wiped the growing smiles off their faces. "What is it, Poppy?" Ingrid asked, looking worried. "What's wrong?"

"It's what Penny said," I replied, "about where Scrimshaw's collection of fossils was."

Ingrid's face paled. "In the town hall," she gasped.

Kip looked from me to Ingrid and back again. "So, what are you saying?" he asked. "That we might have solved the clue but that the next clue was burned up in the fire? We know that's not true because somebody found the second clue, remember." He slumped back against the tree trunk, his hands spread out in front of him like he was reaching for some sort of answer.

"I think it's more than that, Kip," I said slowly. "Think about it. The clue said, 'Set a fire beneath my bones.'"

"You think ... the town hall fire?" Ingrid shuddered, wide-eyed.

"Where did the fire start?" I asked wildly. "On the second floor. *In the exhibition*."

We stood, staring at each other.

"I think someone was following the clue. I think that's why the fire started." I shook my head in disbelief.

There was a pause.

"But there's even more," I said solemnly. "And it's bad."

"What?" Kip asked as Ingrid clutched my arm.

"It's what happened last night ... to Penny," I said. Kip and Ingrid looked at me in surprise. "Penny Farthing ... she's Phineas Scrimshaw's last remaining family member."

Kip looked confused but Ingrid's face was horrified.

"You think someone's ... trying to get rid of Penny?" she whispered. "Because of the gold? That's why they tried to get her to eat the cake with peanuts in?"

I nodded seriously. "The same person who dressed up as a waiter and gave Penny that cake also had the second clue," I said. "If the person who had the second clue started the fire to get it then that means *all* of these things are the work of one person. You guys," I said slowly, "I don't think we've been solving two separate mysteries at all. The fire and the gold, they're joined together. It's been a double mystery all along."

CHAPTER THIRTY-FIVE

"Double, double toil and trouble," muttered Ingrid, a dazed look on her face.

"What?" Kip scrunched his face up in her direction. "Are you all right, Ing?"

"It's from *Macbeth*," Ingrid said in a far away voice. "You're right, Poppy, all along it's been a double mystery, a double jinx! Double trouble, just as the witches in the play say."

"But who is it? Who's looking for the treasure?" asked Kip. "It could be anyone." He groaned.

"And it must have worked," I said, "the fire, I mean. The person who set the fire got the clue. And then they dropped it outside the hall, with the gorilla mask. And that means that burning old

Scrimshaw's fossils must have revealed the second clue somehow."

"I don't get it," Kip exploded. "How could lighting a fire under some bones give you a clue?"

"Maybe there was a message written on the bone?" Ingrid said. "If you want to send secret messages you can write in some special chemicals that are invisible until you heat them up." She paused. "Or I suppose you could have been meant to burn the bones up if there's something hidden inside, but that wouldn't work – not with a real bone, anyway."

"Not with a real bone," I said thoughtfully. "But what if it was made of something else? Something that looked like a bone but which actually held the clue?"

Ingrid wrinkled her nose. "Something that would burn or melt," she said slowly. "Maybe something made of wood or wax or something."

"And it would have been sitting there in his collection all along," breathed Kip. "The key to finding the treasure, right under everyone's noses."

I turned over what Kip and Ingrid had said in my mind. It was like I could almost see the answer but there was a tiny piece missing. A hollow bone. . .

Right under everyone's noses... And then the missing piece clicked into place.

"WAX!" I cried. "That's it! That's why it was so strange."

"What are you talking about, Poppy?" Ingrid asked, bemused.

"I need to get something from our room. Come on!" I ran off towards the girls' dorm and Kip and Ingrid chased after me. At the doorway to the dormitory Kip hesitated.

"There's no one around," I said, "they're all off with their parents – or wrestling guinea pigs!" I grinned, and the three of us rushed in, ran upstairs and pushed open the door to mine and Ingrid's room.

"Ooooh, this is nice," said Kip, looking around. "I think the girls' dorm have nicer curtains."

"We haven't got time for you to appreciate the interior design, Kip!" I exclaimed, diving under my bed. "Where is it?" I flailed around trying to get my hands on the valuable clue. "Eureka!" I cried, emerging triumphantly with Buttons's carry case in my hands. Ingrid was sitting neatly on her bed, flicking through the Phineas Scrimshaw book, no doubt looking for more information. Kip was staring at me like I was a lunatic. I suppose emerging from under your bed clutching a purple leopard-print cat carrier and shouting "Eureka" is not the sanest behaviour.

Putting the case on my bed I carefully opened the little door and peered inside. "Eureka!" I muttered again. "I guess now we know someone wasn't melting candles in here." I pointed inside at the white wax melted into the lining. "Look!"

Kip and Ingrid huddled around and looked where I was pointing. There, in the wax was the perfect imprint of a tiny key. I hadn't noticed it before because it was so small.

"Unbelievable," murmured Ingrid.

"So they melted the wax and found the key," Kip said slowly. "And found the next clue? But why did they melt it in Buttons's carry case?"

"I don't know." I frowned. "But at least now we know how this treasure hunter found the second clue ... and that they have some kind of key to something."

"I've read the book three times now," said Ingrid, waving the Phineas Scrimshaw book in the air. "I can't believe I didn't pick up on the connection to his fossil collection." She shook her head. "Whoever owned this book before it was donated to the library should have done though, by the look of all this green ink."

"What?" I asked.

"The criminal who defaced this antique book. They've written their name in the front, see? They've underlined a bunch of stuff about Scrimshaw's collections." Ingrid pointed to the name. "I can't quite make it out … A. Scoggins? Or Scroggins, maybe?"

"A. Scroggins," I said again, turning the name around in my mind. Why did it sound so familiar? And then suddenly I was struck by a memory, a memory of my conversation with Lucas Quest's mother. "Arthur Scroggins!" I gasped.

"Who?" Kip and Ingrid's faces looked baffled.

"Arthur Scroggins," I repeated. "That's his real name."

"Whose real name?" Kip cried.

"Maxwell Dangerfield," I whispered. "A. Scroggins is Maxwell Dangerfield."

CHAPTER THIRTY-SIX

"Maxwell Dangerfield?" spluttered Kip. "Our Maxwell Dangerfield? That hammy actor? You think he's after Scrimshaw's gold? You think he started the fire?"

"I don't know!" I said. "All I know is that this is his book." I pointed to the name again.

"But we do know something else," said Ingrid, slowly, "remember? We caught him with that painting of Phineas Scrimshaw."

Kip and I turned to look at her. "You're right," I murmured.

"He said it would make a good prop," Kip reminded us.

"But he'd taken it off the wall," said Ingrid, "that's

not something you usually do, is it? With a really old painting that doesn't belong to you?"

"Anyway," I said, "it's a big coincidence, if it was just an innocent interest. Still, this mystery has been so twisty and twirly, I think we need to go and talk to Maxwell. See if we can find out anything else before we tell Inspector Hartley of our suspicions." I turned to my pals. "What do you think?"

Ingrid nodded. "We'll have to ask him some subtle questions at tonight's dress rehearsal."

"Actually," Kip piped up, "he's already here. I saw him on the way to the dining hall. He said he wanted to have the real tour of the school and Mr Grant invited him to the morning session."

I looked at my watch. "Well, that's just about to start! What do you reckon? Shall we try and find out what's going on once and for all?"

"Yes." Kip and Ingrid both nodded solemnly. I felt a tingle in my toes and a thrill of nervous excitement. Perhaps we were finally going to get some answers.

We reached the entrance hall just in time to catch Mr Grant's opening remarks.

"Just keep your eyes peeled!" I muttered, as we huddled in with the other students and their parents.

"There he is!" whispered Ingrid, pointing to Maxwell who was standing near Mr Grant and following him upstairs. At the sight of Maxwell I felt my stomach do a little loop-the-loop. It was all very well being a top-class detective but the big downside was that it did mean that you had to deal with potentially dangerous criminals. I heard Kip make a gulping noise and, looking at his and Ingrid's faces, I realized that the same thought had occurred to them as well. We might well be standing a few feet from someone who started a dangerous fire just to get what he wanted. What would someone like that do to three school kids who got in his way? Did we really want to find out?

So you're just going to leave, are you? a stern voice in my head asked. *Are you really going to walk away from a mystery like this? Leave the case unsolved? Is that what Dougie Valentine would do?* I dug deep inside myself for all the scraps of courage that I could find and straightened my shoulders. I gave Kip and Ingrid a stern and flinty-eyed look that was meant to communicate with them that we could DO this, that we were *professionals*. It must have worked a little bit because Ingrid gave me a weak smile and Kip stood up a bit straighter. (In fact, he looked a good half a centimetre taller and I made a mental note to tell him so later.)

We smushed in tighter with the tour group and moved along the staircase with them. Mr Grant had stopped, like yesterday, in front of the portrait of Phineas Scrimshaw. My eyes swivelled to Maxwell's face. He was watching Mr Grant carefully.

"This painting is a portrait of Lord Phineas Scrimshaw, the last owner of Saint Smithen's before it became a school," Mr Grant said, Maxwell's eyes never once wavering from his face. Then Maxwell raised his hand and Mr Grant looked surprised. "Yes?" he said. "Do you have a question?"

Kip, Ingrid and I exchanged significant looks.

"It's a wonderful painting," Maxwell said with his toothy smile on display. "Has it always hung here on the staircase? It's a bit wasted, hidden away here."

"Actually, no," said Mr Grant, and although Maxwell's smile remained in place, his eyes seemed to flare with excitement. "It used to hang in the great hall, over the fireplace I believe, but it was moved to make room for the school's portrait of Saint Smithen."

"Aaah," said Maxwell smoothly, "very interesting."

Mr Grant turned back to the painting and

continued talking. With a tiny glance either side of him, Maxwell began edging out of the group and up the stairs. In a couple of seconds he had rounded the bend and was headed for the third floor.

"Come on!" I exclaimed, "Quick!", and we, too, edged our way around the group, heading after him. When we reached the third floor it was to see Maxwell disappearing up the stairs to the attic.

"Let's follow him," I whispered.

Ingrid nodded.

"Follow the suspect into the spooky attic?!" hooted Kip. "Great idea. Haven't either of you ever read a book? Let's just wait for him to come back down."

"But we could be missing something important!" I said urgently. "I'm going."

"Fine," said Kip, "we'll all go. But don't say I didn't warn you!"

And with that the three of us crept slowly up into the attic.

CHAPTER THIRTY-SEVEN

The attic was a gloomy room, the only light coming from a small skylight way up in the high ceiling. All around us bulky objects were covered with dustsheets, and the air was thick and musty. The three of us huddled together inside the doorway and moved cautiously into the room.

"What now, Poppy?" whispered Kip.

"My question exactly, Miss Pym," came a voice from behind us. We whipped around to find Maxwell Dangerfield standing between us and the open door. With a terrible finality he pushed the door shut behind him. "What exactly is going on here?" he asked silkily, and I noticed that he was holding several large black canvas bags in his hand. He must have stashed his looting kit up here.

"You've found it!" I burst out, before I could stop myself. "You know where the gold is, don't you!?"

Maxwell's eyes narrowed and he didn't look as friendly as usual. In fact, as he took a step towards us, he looked positively menacing. "Well, you three have been busy." His voice was charming as always, but his eyes were icy cold. His right hand moved to his hip and from his belt he pulled a glimmering silver dagger, which he pointed at us. "Now, why don't you tell me what you know?"

"N-nothing," I stuttered. "We don't know anything."

"It's true," squeaked Kip, "we know nothing. Absolutely nothing. About anything. Just ask us. We don't even know the capital of Sweden, do we, Ingrid?"

"Well, Stockholm is the capital of Sweden," Ingrid said nervously. "But about all of *this*, it's true that we know very little."

Maxwell took a step towards us. "Leave the acting to the professionals, children." He waved the dagger towards me. "You! Tell me!"

I swallowed. "We know you started the fire," I

whispered, and Maxwell's face tightened. "And we know you found the key in the bone. That's it."

"Well that's much more than I wanted anyone to know," Maxwell growled. "The fire was an accident. I had a candle and was trying it underneath each of the fossils, and when I found that one of the bones was made of wax and it began to melt ... well, in my excitement I dropped the candle. The room was so full of ancient knick-knacks and old papers and what-not that it all went up in flames before I knew what was happening."

"But if it was an accident," I gasped, "can't you just tell the police that?"

"Oh, and share all the treasure I'm about to uncover, I suppose?!" Maxwell snapped. "Have you forgotten that there's still a Scrimshaw heir living in Brimwell?"

"Penny!" I shuddered. "Then it *was* you in the gorilla mask. You were trying to get rid of her."

"Oh very clever!" mocked Maxwell. "You think I'm going to share this fortune with that crazy cat lady after all the hard work I've put in to find it? No, thank you! I was fascinated by the treasure even as a young boy."

"We know. We found your book," Ingrid said

shakily. "*The Secret Life of Phineas Scrimshaw.* You wrote your name in the front." She gulped. "Your real name."

Maxwell glared at her. "I wondered where that had disappeared to," he said. "I assumed it got donated somewhere when they cleared out my parents' house in Brimwell. I'd almost forgotten all about the treasure when I was off being a successful actor. And then I found myself cast out, back in Brimwell, broke and unappreciated. Then, when I was working on this crummy production in the town hall I saw the exhibition and it all clicked. It was my fate, my destiny. I was the one who would solve the mystery that had baffled generations of treasure hunters." His face was shining now, lit from the skylight high above.

"But how does the cat-carrier come in?" I couldn't resist asking.

"Oh, you found that, did you? You're quite the little detectives, aren't you?" He laughed humourlessly. "Yes, well that wasn't exactly a part of the plan but then neither was the fire. I had to adapt quickly. The bone was bigger than I had calculated, and the wax was melting everywhere in the heat of the fire. I couldn't very well walk out of a burning building carrying a half-melted bone now, could I? I was trying to be inconspicuous. Then I saw my chance to get the bone out and to rid myself of Penny in one go. I let the cat out, stuffed the bone in, and walked out of the building. If anyone asked I could say that I thought I was saving Penny's stupid cat – that I didn't realize the *poor* creature had got out." He batted his eyes innocently. "I stashed the carrier round the corner where I could pick it up later. I knew Penny was stupid enough to go running into the fire after that mangy cat, and with the last Scrimshaw heir out of the way, the gold would be all mine. Then that firefighter caught her trying to get back in, and you had to step in and save the day." He shot me a poisonous glare.

"You would have let Penny go back into that fire?" I asked, horrified.

"Don't look so shocked," Maxwell barked. "I would have let her choke to death from a peanut too. I did what I had to do, don't you see?"

"And the portrait?" Kip asked desperately. "What has that got to do with anything?"

Maxwell laughed again. "The first clue led to the bone, and once I'd melted that I found the second clue inside with a key."

"We found it," I managed, and Maxwell paused with a surprised look on his face. "The second clue, I mean. It was screwed up next to the gorilla mask. We found the tree but the clue was already gone."

"Another careless mistake," snapped Maxwell, "but no matter. No harm done in the end. After all, here you are and now I am about to go and take my treasure." His eyes glistened dangerously.

"Wait!" I said desperately. "What about the final clue? What was hidden beneath the tree?"

In response Maxwell threw his head back, and recited in his best acting voice (by which I mean he recited it very loudly):

"Riddle me three, the last of all,
Pride does come before a fall,
Behind the likeness of this lord
You shall unlock your just reward."

"The gold's behind the painting!" Kip yelled.

"Only it's not," I said quietly. "Because the painting was moved. The gold is in the great hall, behind the fireplace."

"Excellent deduction, Miss Pym!" Maxwell sneered. "And of course I have the key that was hidden inside the bone to open the secret door . . .

which I am going to do right now." He moved backwards towards the door.

"Right now?" I squeaked desperately. "In the middle of the day?"

Maxwell smirked. "Of course! The hall is empty for the next hour thanks to your school's thoroughly well organized timetable of events, and if anyone asks about my presence or my bags I can just tell them I'm sorting out the props for the play. No one will even question the presence of a big star like me. It's called hiding in plain sight." Maxwell's smile was stretched right across his face now. "But I'm afraid this is one performance you three are going to have to miss. By the time anyone even thinks of looking for you, me and my gold will be long gone."

"You won't get away with this!" railed Kip, shaking his fist.

Maxwell sneered. "Actually, I rather think I will. One can do an awful lot with a big fortune, you know. Go anywhere, be whoever you like, even forge a new identity. They'll never find me. For a great actor like myself, nothing could be easier. It will be the role of a lifetime!" He bowed theatrically in the doorway – and stumbled slightly as he straightened up.

With that he let himself out through the door and pushed it closed behind him. We rushed forward, but it was too late. With a chilling click he locked us in. And his echoing footsteps trailed down the staircase into silence.

CHAPTER THIRTY-EIGHT

We rattled the handle and banged on the door and yelled as loudly as we could, but it was no good, Maxwell was right – nobody could hear us. We were trapped!

A wave of panic seemed to rush up from my toes, leaving my skin tingling.

"What are we going to do?" Ingrid whispered.

"If we don't get out of here, he'll be long gone with the gold!" I exclaimed, trying hard to think straight.

"I hate to say I told you so, but—" Kip stopped when Ingrid and I swivelled around with fire in our eyes. "OK, OK," he said, holding up his hands, "We need an escape plan."

We all looked around the room but there were no windows or doors other than the one tiny skylight.

"We have to go up there," I said, pointing up at it, and looking around for something to climb. "Help me stack those boxes."

"How will we ever get out that way?" Kip asked.

"We'll climb over the roof," I said. Kip and Ingrid looked at me in horror. "OK," I said, "*I'll* climb over the roof and then I'll come back and let you out."

It wasn't the best or clearest plan but it was all that we had. We began stacking boxes until we had a reasonable tower, but it was soon clear it wasn't going to be enough. "We'll never get them high enough," I panted. "Not the ones we can lift, anyway." I looked at the height, calculating how far off we still were. "Human tower!" I said finally.

"Er, human what now?" Kip asked.

"We'll have to go up on each other's shoulders," I said briskly. "Come on."

I climbed on top of the boxes. "Who's going on the bottom?" I asked. "It needs to be the strongest person."

"I'm going on the bottom," Kip yelled, striding manfully forward. "I am the strongest. The sprouts won't fail me now!"

"OK," I said with a nod. "Ingrid, get on Kip's shoulders."

Ingrid began clambering on to Kip's shoulders, but she looked far from pleased.

"Gah! Ingrid!" Kip exclaimed, swaying beneath her weight. "What have you been eating, rocks?"

"That's very rude!" murmured Ingrid. "And I don't think *you* should be talking about how much people eat!"

"What?" Kip looked puzzled. "I hardly eat anything."

"OK," I interrupted, "we're nearly there. Steady yourselves. Now I just have to climb on to Ingrid's shoulders."

"Uggggh!" groaned Kip as I put a foot in his hand. "You've definitely been eating rocks, Poppy. It's a good job I'm really, *really* strong or this would probably be very difficult." His voice was getting a bit shaky now.

"You're doing great," I said, finally climbing on to Ingrid's shoulders. I reached up but we were still short of the skylight. "OK, I need to stand up now," I said.

"What?!" said Ingrid, and for a moment the tower swayed precariously.

"It's fine," I said, "I do this all the time. We're nearly there!" I carefully clambered up so that my feet were on Ingrid's shoulders and I reached up. "So . . . close!" I gasped. "Everyone stretch!"

"Aaaaaargh!" we all groaned and I reached up again. It was closer but still too far. For a moment the tower wobbled and I thought we would fall, but we regained our balance and I cried down, "One last push!"

Then below me I heard a big intake of breath and a cry of "SPROUT POWER!" and felt myself slowly rising up towards the ceiling. I reached up and pushed the skylight open.

"We've got it!" I cried, hooking my hands over the edge as Kip and Ingrid promptly crumpled into a heap on the floor. I hung on, my legs dangling in the air. With a big pull I heaved myself up through the tiny window and found myself up on a flat section of the roof. Kneeling, I stuck my face back through the skylight. "Are you two OK?" I called.

Kip and Ingrid got gingerly to their feet. "I think so," Ingrid called. "Can you get down somehow?"

I looked around me. I was very high up, on the highest part of the school's higgledy-piggledy roof. "I think I can see a way," I shouted. "I'll get someone to come and let you out in a minute."

"OK, Poppy," I heard them call. "Be careful!"

I took a deep breath and began to climb down the sloping shingles until I came to a section of the roof where a big gap was linked only by a long, thin pipe. I bent down and felt the pipe to see if it would hold my weight and then telling myself *Don't look down*, I stepped out, my arms held out either side for balance, and inched across to the other side. Now I was down level with the second floor windows. I stepped on to the first ledge and peered inside, but all that I could see was a dark classroom and the window would not open. Another classroom lay over to my left and I saw with a jolt that the window was slightly open. But to get to the next window ledge I would have to somehow clamber across the big gap between the windows with nothing to stand on. I looked at the stonework and saw only a sheer drop, down, down, down to the hard ground below.

My heart beat faster. What could I do? The criminal was getting away! I knew what I had to do, I just wasn't sure if I could do it without getting splattered. I could feel panic rising inside me and my breath was coming in short, sharp bursts but I had to get inside the school somehow. I gripped the stonework as best as I could with my hands and stepped off the window ledge. I started moving painfully slowly, hand over hand, towards the open window to my left. My hands hurt as I clung to the rough stonework, my feet continually slipped as I tried to find a foothold between the stones. I was halfway across the gap when things started to go very wrong.

"Poppy!" I heard someone shriek far below me.

Craning my neck I saw Miss Baxter standing below me, with a growing crowd.

"Inspector Hartley!" I shouted. He was standing next to Miss Baxter, looking up at me. "Maxwell Dangerfield! He started the fire! He's in the great hall!" I shouted as loudly as I could, but I could feel my left hand was starting to slip. In agonizing slow motion one finger after another was peeling away from the wall.

"Poppy!" I heard my name again, but this time it was Pym's voice.

"Pym!" I screamed, feeling my hand losing its grip completely. I was hanging on now by the fingers of my right hand, scrabbling with the other to find something to hold on to. All my muscles were burning and I realized that this time I had gone too far. My toe found a tiny hole in the stonework and I clung as tightly as I could, but I felt the fingers on my right hand start to slip as well.

Suddenly, Tina and Tawna sprang forward from the group and their acrobatic skills were dazzling as they leapt up the walls, throwing Pym, tumbling, between them. Before I even really knew what was happening they were up level with me. Tina was hanging upside down, on my right, her legs hooked over a drainpipe, her hands holding on to Tawna's feet.

Across from her, on my left, Pym was also hanging from the window sill, reaching out her hand for me. I stretched out with the fingers of the hand not holding on to the wall, but it was no use. I couldn't reach her. I whimpered in fright.

"Poppy," Pym's voice reached me. "Don't be scared. I'm going to get you, OK?" She said it in her firm voice, the one you can't argue with. I nodded, but I could feel my one-handed grasp on the wall slipping.

"Tina is going to swing Tawna towards you, and you're going to grab her hand with your free hand. And then Tawna's going to swing you to me and I'm going to catch you. Just like we've done a hundred times before, OK?" she asked, and we all nodded.

"Go!" she shouted, and Tawna swung forward and grabbed my free hand. "Now let go, Poppy. I've got you!" Pym shouted as my hand began to slip through Tawna's fingers. Tawna flung me forward as hard as she could. I sailed across the gap, reaching out my hands towards Pym, and the crowd below us gasped.

I knew with a horrible certainty that the trick would fail, just as it had in my nightmare, and I closed my eyes as I tumbled through the air.

Then I felt Pym's fingers closing tightly around mine and I heard her voice in my ear. "I've got you, lovey," she said.

The world seemed to wobble a bit around me and the next thing I knew Pym was pulling me up on to the windowsill and into a shaky hug.

Below us the sound of cheering filled the air, and I heard the creaking sound of a window being pushed open.

"And what mess have you got yourself into now, Poppy?" A voice drifted through the window and a familiar face appeared. I didn't think I'd ever be so happy to see Miss Susan.

CHAPTER THIRTY-NINE

Miss Susan pulled me through the window and for a brief moment I stood shaking with her arms around me. I could feel the speedy beating of her heart, and my cheek was pressed against something cool and metallic. A necklace. My foggy thoughts were trying to put something together but finally my detective instincts kicked in.

"Maxwell Dangerfield!" I cried, breaking away from Miss Susan. I began to run for the stairs but my legs were still wobbling like nervous bowls of jelly. *Come on, Poppy!* I said to myself, sternly. *Everyone's counting on you. Would Dougie Valentine be slowed down by a little near-death experience?!* I gulped and thought that maybe the author of the

Dougie Valentine books hadn't had their own near-death experience or there might be a bit more knee-knocking and a bit less LAUGHING IN THE FACE OF DANGER. I staggered down the stairs as fast as I could, bumping into people in my hurry. "And someone needs to let Kip and Ingrid out of the attic!" I called over my shoulder to a very confused-looking Miss Susan and Pym.

By the time I burst through the doors to the great hall I was feeling much sturdier, and I found Maxwell Dangerfield slumped on the floor being handcuffed by Inspector Hartley. "But I was so close!" he screeched, drumming his feet against the ground like an angry toddler. "I would have got it all if it hadn't been for YOU!" His venomous eyes snapped in my direction, full to the brim of violent hatred. He began to struggle to his feet, lunging towards me, but Inspector Hartley grabbed him by the shoulder, tugging him back to the ground.

"That will do, thank you, Mr Scroggins," the inspector said coolly. "As I mentioned before, you do have the right to remain silent and I suggest you make use of it."

"OOOOOh!" Maxwell whimpered. "So close to the gold! If you will only let me find the keyhole –

just let me look at it!" He scrabbled, trying to get to his feet once more. His eyes were wide and pleading, and his tone wheedling and whiny. The inspector just ignored him.

"Perhaps you would like to do the honours, Miss Pym?" Inspector Hartley said, pressing something into my hand. It was a very small gold key. "I just confiscated this from Mr Dangerfield after a very interesting chat. I'm afraid he'll be too busy doing time in prison for arson and attempted murder to do much treasure-seeking from now on."

With a tremendous THUD, the door to the great hall swung open once more and Kip and Ingrid burst in breathlessly. "DID YOU FIND THE GOLD?" bellowed Kip, bright red in the face from running.

"I think we're just about to," I whispered shakily, and I walked over to the enormous fireplace.

It was tall enough so that I could stand inside it (if I had wanted to stand in a sooty fireplace for some reason), and all around the edges were beautiful figures carved into the stonework. There were all sorts of animals – birds and rabbits and deer and foxes chasing one another around, through a scene of flowers and leaves. It was truly beautiful, and I couldn't believe I had never really looked at it before. I ran my hands over the intricate carvings but I couldn't find the keyhole. Kip and Ingrid were by my side, peering intently at the fireplace but I began to feel a sense of rising panic. What if, after all this, we were in the wrong place? What if there was no keyhole?

Then, finally, just when I had almost given up hope, I spotted it. Right in the middle of a delicate flower, I spotted a tiny hole. I almost laughed when I realized that the flower was a poppy. It felt like a joke between me and Phineas Scrimshaw. As if the treasure hunt was meant for me all along, as if a part of Saint Smithen's had belonged to me the whole time. Holding my breath, I pushed the key inside the hole and turned it with a tiny click.

With an enormous groan the entire fireplace began to move towards us. Kip, Ingrid and I jumped back as, with a loud creaking and cracking noise, it came to a stop.

"What now?" asked Kip.

Tentatively I went to the side of the fireplace. Now that it had moved forward it looked almost like ... a door. I put both hands on the side and puuuullllllllllled.

The crowd of parents and students that had been drawn to the room by all the commotion stood behind the inspector and Maxwell, and as the door swung open everyone gasped.

CHAPTER FORTY

Behind the door was a hidden room.

And it was empty.

I stepped cautiously inside the secret room. It was small and square with stone walls. Lying in the middle of the stone floor was an envelope, caked in dust. Gingerly I picked it up and dusted it off. The faded ink on the front said:

To the Treasure Seeker

I tore open the envelope with shaking hands and gently unfolded the delicate paper inside. In a slightly trembly voice I read the words aloud.

To the Seeker of old Scrimshaw's gold,

I warned you, did I not, that pride came before a fall? This is a lesson I know all too well. The truth is, I have no fortune. I wasted most of what I had as a youth, and that which was left I lost in a bad investment, though I was too proud to admit it. And so I have pretended to live out my final years as a miser, concealing my true poverty with my penny-pinching ways. If you have arrived at this place seeking gold I am afraid I must disappoint you. I set this treasure hunt as an act of revenge against a family that cared nothing for one another, only for material wealth. I hope that you, who find this letter, have the wisdom to know that the person who has a family that offers love and affection is truly rich beyond belief, and possesses a gift more precious than any gold.

Your faithful servant,

Phineas Scrimshaw.

"You mean, it was a trick?" Maxwell Dangerfield's cry fractured the heavy silence. "All this for ... nothing?! The years of research... All this planning! The scheming!" He began to laugh hysterically until fat tears were rolling down his cheeks.

"Yes," I said quietly. "It was all a trick. One that was meant for cruel, greedy people like you. It serves you right." I turned to the crown. "This man is Arthur Scroggins." I pointed to him. "He started the fire at the town hall and he tried to kill Penny Farthing ... twice. All to get his hands on the Scrimshaw gold."

"Don't you call me that name!" he screeched, lurching towards me once more. "I'm Maxwell Dangerfield and I'm a star!" He turned to face his horrified audience. "I'm a star," he repeated in a whisper, falling to the ground.

"Yes, Mr Scroggins," Inspector Hartley agreed. "I'm sure you'll be the star of many an amateur production in prison. Which is where you're headed, for a long time," and with that Inspector Hartley dragged him to his feet and led him away while the crowd cheered.

I stood with the dusty letter in my hand and felt dozens of eyes on me.

Looking up I saw Pym watching me with a broad smile. She held her arms up and I ran into them. It was a long hug and the rest of my family soon joined in. Phineas Scrimshaw's letter twirled around my head and I realized suddenly that it wasn't words like "mum" or "dad" that mattered. Families might look completely different but having people that love and care for you is what is really important. A lot of people didn't have that, but I did. Phineas Scrimshaw was right, at that moment I felt like the richest girl in the world.

"Well," said Miss Baxter, dabbing at her eyes with a hankie, "I should say we could all do with a nice cup of tea and a biscuit. Ladies and gentlemen, if you'd like to follow me to the dining hall."

"Ah. Small problem there, Miss B," said Marvin with a guilty smile. "Think I may have left my hat open again," he said nervously, "and those little fluffy fellows caught the scent of the biscuit buffet. There was no budging them after that."

Pym looked like she was about to strongly disagree, when she was interrupted by Fanella. "Coward Marvin surrender dining hall to guinea pig army," she smirked with her arms folded across her chest. "He no listen to me when I tell him retreat is showing them weakness."

"But Fanella," said Luigi reasonably, "you know it was the only way to reach a peaceful solution."

"Bah!" said Fanella.

"Right, well, I think you'd better go and sort it out, hadn't you?" Pym gave Marvin a stern look.

"Yes, yes," he spluttered. "Come on then, troops!" and he led the crowd of performers, parents and students off to face down their ferocious enemy.

Pym caught me by the arm so that we stayed behind, alone, in the great hall.

"Another case closed." She looked at me with a funny expression in her scrunched-up eye. "But . . . perhaps . . . there's another mystery for Poppy Pym to solve?" She pulled the brown envelope out of her pocket. In all the excitement I had almost forgotten about it. Almost.

"If anyone can solve it, you can." Pym gave me a big squeezing hug, and without another word she left to join the others. I loved that she knew just when I needed to be by myself.

From the dining hall I heard faint cries of, "Stop the guinea pigs! Attack!" and with shaking hands I opened the envelope again.

I tipped the envelope and the necklace fell into

my hand. I looked again at the delicate chain with tiny pearls threaded on to it, and the dainty silver heart-shaped charm with a feeling of shock growing in my belly. I pressed the heart to my cheek and felt the cool metal there, just as I had felt it only a few minutes ago. With a sob, I realized where I had seen the necklace before.

Around Miss Susan's neck.

EPILOGUE

That Halloween, Brimwell saw the funniest version of *Macbeth* ever performed. Here's a clipping from the *Brimwell Bugle*.

It was a triumph! I have not previously picked up on the comedy that runs rampant through *Macbeth*, and I will never look at Shakespeare the same way again. Particular highlights included the actor playing Macbeth (or Boris as he preferred to be known for completely plausible reasons of plot), who was most affecting. Also special praise must go to the spectacular Lady M herself, who brought a keen ear to the language of the play, and introduced the audience to a totally new experience of the Bard's poetry. In truth the production was almost stolen by the army of guinea pig soldiers in tiny uniforms, something this reporter has certainly never seen before.

ACKNOWLEDGEMENTS

There are so many people to thank but I would like to begin with my brilliant family. Thanks to my parents and my brother for being so supportive and for believing all of this would happen from the very beginning. A special thanks and a 'What-Ho!' to UM, the real-life Luigi. I must thank Mick, Carole and John for being so wonderful and for whisking me off to France where this book began, I am so lucky that you are my family! To the Wellers, of course, and ESPECIALLY to Imogen and Alex who designed Miss Marigold's cake trolley and filled it with the best of imaginary baked goods. As with all the good things in my life, this just wouldn t be possible without Paul Grigsby – my best friend and my comedy name generator. He still thinks all the best bits were his idea.

I would like to thank Giuseppe, Charles, Nina and the rest of the team at Montegrappa for their continuing support and encouragement as well as for the truly beautiful pen that wrote most of the words in this book. I would also like to thank the Institute of Advanced Studies at the University of Warwick. I wrote the first draft of this book while I was a part of their Early Career Fellowship programme and the support that I received was overwhelming. Thank you all so much for the important work you do.

To my agent Louise, who knows better than anyone the small but pivotal role of Macduff's son, thank you for ALL you have done in bringing this book into being. Thanks to Lena and Gen, an editing dream team, working with both of you on this book will always make it particularly special. A million thank-yous to Samuel Perrett and Beatrice Bencivenni who have brought both Poppy books to life with their talent and enthusiasm, and to the rest of the team at Scholastic for making my words into this beautiful book - you are the best.

Finally, I would like to acknowledge a group of particularly brilliant and beautiful women.

To Laura, Alice C-H, Alice G, Anna, Sarah, Suse, Rosie, Jess, and Emma, thank you for making writing about funny and clever school friends so easy. And to our newest member, Polly Parker, welcome to our gang – it's a good one.

ABOUT THE AUTHOR

Laura Wood won the inaugural Montegrappa Scholastic Prize for New Children's Writing with her first novel, *Poppy Pym and the Pharaoh's Curse*. Since then, she has been shortlisted for the Sainsbury's Children's Book Award and is currently working on more books in the Poppy Pym series. Laura has recently completed her PhD in English Literature at the University of Warwick. She loves Georgette Heyer novels, Fred Astaire films, travelling to far-flung places, recipe books, cosy woollen jumpers, crisp autumn leaves, new stationery, salted caramel, dogs, and drinking lashings of ginger beer.

Like I said, if you haven't read
my first book you really definitely should.

Look at all of these great reviews!

"I foretell that you will love this book"
*Madame Pym, prognosticator, predictionist
and all around mind-reader*

"Simply smashing"
Luigi, lion tamer

"Rooooooar"
Buttercup, the Lion

"★ ★ ★ ★ ★"
The Magnificent Marvin

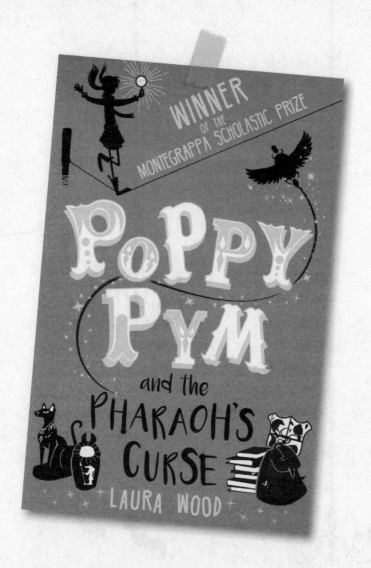

WINNER
OF THE
MONTEGRAPPA SCHOLASTIC PRIZE

POPPY
PYM
and the
PHARAOH'S
CURSE
LAURA WOOD

(It's shiny and gold and you will totally LOVE it!)

Love, Poppy xx